Back by Popular Demand

A collector's edition of favorite titles from
one of the world's best-loved romance
authors. Harlequin is proud to bring
back these sought-after titles and present
them as one cherished collection.

BETTY NEELS:
COLLECTOR'S EDITION

A GENTLE AWAKENING
RING IN A TEACUP
OFF WITH THE OLD LOVE
THE MOON FOR LAVINIA
PINEAPPLE GIRL
BRITANNIA ALL AT SEA
CAROLINE'S WATERLOO
HEAVEN AROUND THE CORNER
THE LITTLE DRAGON
THE SILVER THAW
ALL ELSE CONFUSION
NEVER SAY GOODBYE
THE PROMISE OF HAPPINESS
A GIRL TO LOVE
A DREAM CAME TRUE
NEVER TOO LATE

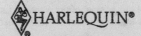

HARLEQUIN®

Betty Neels spent her childhood and youth in Devonshire before training as a nurse and midwife. She was an army nursing sister during the war, married a Dutchman and subsequently lived in Holland for fourteen years. She now lives with her husband in Dorset, and has a daughter and grandson. Her hobbies are reading, animals, old buildings and, of course, writing. Betty started to write on retirement from nursing, incited by a lady in a library bemoaning the lack of romantic novels.

Mrs. Neels is always delighted to receive fan letters, but would truly appreciate it if they could be directed to Harlequin Mills & Boon Ltd., 18-24 Paradise Road, Richmond, Surrey, TW9 1SR, England.

Books by Betty Neels

BETTY NEELS

A GIRL TO LOVE

COLLECTOR'S EDITION

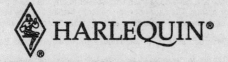

HARLEQUIN®

TORONTO • NEW YORK • LONDON
AMSTERDAM • PARIS • SYDNEY • HAMBURG
STOCKHOLM • ATHENS • TOKYO • MILAN • MADRID
PRAGUE • WARSAW • BUDAPEST • AUCKLAND

ISBN 0-373-63114-6

A GIRL TO LOVE

First North American Publication 1999.

Copyright © 1982 by Betty Neels.

CHAPTER ONE

THE COTTAGE STOOD sideways on to the lane, its wicket gate opening on to a narrow brick path between flower beds, the path ending at an old-fashioned door with a round brass knob and a great knocker. Its thatched roof above cob walls was much patched, although picturesque, and doubtless in the summer it presented a charming picture, but just now, on a dripping November afternoon, it looked forlorn, as forlorn as the girl opening the gate.

She was wrapped in a rather elderly raincoat with a scarf wound round her neck and a woolly cap pulled well down on to a pale face, quite unremarkable save for a pair of fine dark eyes, and despite the bulky coat, she was too thin. She closed the gate carefully, hurried up the path and let herself into the cottage, casting off her outdoor things in the hall and going straight into the sitting room.

It was a pleasant enough room with some nice pieces furnishing it and a scattering of shabby armchairs. The girl switched on the light, scooped up the sleek cat sitting in one of the chairs and with him on her lap, sat down. The room was untidy and across the hall the dining room table was still littered with cups and saucers and plates and the remains of cake and sandwiches consumed by friends who had attended the funeral and returned for tea afterwards. But that would have to wait. The girl had too much on her mind to bother about washing up for the moment; she'd had a shock and she needed to go over every word Mr Banks the solicitor had said to her before she could face up to it.

The funeral had been well attended. Granny had no family except herself left, but many friends, and they had all come; it had been a busy day, and it was only when the last of them had gone and only Mr Banks was left that she had felt a pang of loneliness. At his suggestion that they should sit and have a talk for a while she had felt better and she had sat down opposite him, not surprised when he had said kindly: 'Sadie, there is the will…'

She had nodded, not over interested; she had lived with her grandmother since she was a very small girl and although there had never been much money she knew that the cottage would be hers. Her grandmother's pension died with her, but there was always a living to be earned. She had wanted to get a job after she had left school, but her grandmother wouldn't hear of it, so although at twenty-three she was a skilled housewife, a splendid cook and a clever needlewoman, she wasn't trained for

anything else, and she had never thought about it
much, especially during the last two years when
Granny had been so crippled with arthritis that she
had been forced to give up active life and depend
entirely on Sadie.

Mr Banks unfolded the will and cleared his
throat. Mrs Gillard had left all that she possessed
to her granddaughter. But there was more to it than
that; he folded the will up tidily and blew his nose,
reluctant to speak. When he did, Sadie didn't believe him at first. The cottage was mortgaged up to
the hilt—Granny had been living on the money for
some years, for her pension hadn't gone up as
wages had, and what had been a respectable income
thirty years ago had dwindled to a mockery of itself... 'So I am very afraid,' said Mr Banks apol-
ogetically, 'that there is no money at all, Sadie, and
the cottage will have to be sold in order to pay off
the mortgage.'

She had looked at him in vague disbelief and he
hastened to add: 'Your grandmother had a few
pounds in some shares. I'll see that they are sold
later, in the meantime I'll advance you their value.'

She had thanked him politely. 'I don't think I
could bear to leave here,' she had told him, and
then at his pitying look: 'But of course I must,
mustn't I? I'll get some sort of job.'

Mr Banks had looked uneasy. 'Can you type? Do shorthand? I might know of someone...'

'I can't do anything like that. I can cook and sew and do the housework. I'll find something.' She had made a great effort and smiled at him. 'Don't worry, Mr Banks, I'll get a job as a housekeeper or mother's help, then I'll have a home and a job.' And before he could protest: 'I'll walk down to the village with you—you left the car at the Bull and Judge, didn't you?'

So she had seen him safely away and now she was back in the cottage which was no longer her house. She had a little time, Mr Banks had assured her, she would be given a week or two to make her plans and move out before the mortgage was foreclosed; and Mr Banks had pointed out that there was the chance that a buyer might be found for the cottage and the mortgage paid off, leaving her a little money besides.

She sat stroking the cat, searching her mind for a likely buyer, but there was no one in the village who would want it; it was a fair-sized place as cottages went, with good-sized rooms, an old-fashioned but adequate kitchen, four bedrooms and an attic as well as a bathroom, as out of date as the kitchen but still functioning, and besides there were a number of pantries and cupboards and a fair-sized garden. But it needed a new thatch and new paint, and the wallpaper had been on the walls ever since she could remember.

She got up presently and started on the washing up and when that was done, tidied the rooms, raked out the fire and took herself off to bed, with Tom the cat for company. The cottage was dreadfully empty without Granny. She hadn't got used to that yet, and her grief went deep, for she had loved the old lady dearly, but she had plenty of good sense; life had to go on and she must make the most of it. She closed her eyes on the thought, but not before a few tears had trickled from under their lids.

Nothing seemed so bad in the morning. It was a cold grey day, but once the fire was lighted and she had had her breakfast and fed Tom, she set about cleaning the cottage. She wasn't sure, but presumably someone would come to look at it. Whoever held the mortgage would want to know its value and they would send someone from a house agents.

There was no telephone in the cottage, so she would have no warning. Charlie Beard the postman came soon after breakfast, propping his bike against the old may tree by the gate and accepting a cup of tea while she looked through the handful of letters he gave her. Her heart sank at the bills—electricity, the last load of coal, the rates… When Charlie had gone she went through all the drawers in the hope of finding some money Granny might have tucked away, and was rewarded by a few pounds in an envelope, and these, added to what she had in her purse, would just about pay for the coal. She wasn't too worried about food; there were vegetables in the garden, potatoes stored in the shed at the end of the garden; eggs could be exchanged with cabbages any time with Mrs Coffin at the end of the lane...and Mr Banks had said that he would send her the money for the shares. It could be worse, she told herself bracingly. Of course, there were any number of vague thoughts at the back of her head. The furniture—would she have to sell it or would it be taken over with the cottage? And Tom? Tom would have to go with her wherever she went; he was too old to have another owner, although she couldn't imagine him living in any other house but the cottage.

She finished tidying the house and went into the garden. There were potatoes to bring in and sprouts to pick as well as the apples stored in the outhouse. Because it was drizzling still she put on the old mac which had hung behind the kitchen door for she didn't know how long, and pulled on her wellies, and while she was out there, since she was wet anyway, she stayed for a while tidying the flower beds in the front garden. There was nothing much in them now, a few chrysanthemums, very bedraggled, and the rose bushes, bare now of all but a handful of soggy leaves. Sadie pottered about until dinner time and after her meal, knowing that it would have to be done sooner or later, started to sort out her grandmother's clothes and small possessions. It was dark by the time she had finished, packing everything away tidily in an old trunk she had dragged down the narrow little stairs which led to the attic at the top of the house. And after tea, for something to do, she went from room to room to room, inspecting each of the four bedrooms carefully to make sure that they were as attractive as possible, and then downstairs to do the same in the dining room and sitting room, and lastly the kitchen, for surely she would hear something tomorrow, either from Mr Banks or from the house agents.

There was a letter from Mr Banks in the morning, but beyond the modest sum, the proceeds from the shares, which was enclosed, he had nothing to say—indeed, day followed day and nothing happened. Sadie went down to the village on the third morning to cash the money order and buy groceries and submit to the kindly questions of Mrs Beamish, the postmistress, and several other ladies in the shop. She didn't mind the questions, she had known them all her life; they weren't being curious, only sympathetic and kind, pressing her to go to tea, offering her a lift in the car next time its owner was going to Bridport, asking if she could do with half a dozen eggs. It was nice to know she had so many friends. She went back to the cottage feeling quite cheerful and after her dinner sat down and composed a letter to Mr Banks, asking him if there was any news about the cottage being sold; she was aware that selling a house took time, but almost a week had gone by and surely he would have something to tell her by now. She finished her letter and was addressing the envelope when she heard the creak of the gate and looked out to see Mr Banks coming up the path.

Mr Banks, a rather dour-looking man although kindly, greeted her so cheerfully that she immediately asked: 'Oh, have you heard something?' and then seeing that he wasn't going to answer for the moment, added quickly: 'Let me have your coat, Mr Banks—how nice to see you, only it's a wretched day for you to be out. Come and sit by the fire and I'll make tea.'

'A most miserable day, Sadie,' he agreed, 'and a cup of tea will be most welcome.'

She went into the kitchen and made the tea in a fever of impatience, then made small talk while they drank it, answering his questions politely while she longed for him to get to the point. Yes, Mr Frobisher the vicar had been to see her, and yes, she had answered almost all the letters she had received when her grandmother had died, and yes, she still had some of the money which he had sent her for the shares. 'But I paid all the bills,' she pointed out, 'so at least I don't owe anything, Mr Banks.'

'Splendid, splendid. And now I have good news for you. Through a colleague of mine I have been in touch with someone who is looking most anxiously for just such a place as this—a playwright, and I believe something to do with television. He is a widower with two children who have a governess and he lives in Highgate Village, but he is seeking somewhere very quiet where he can work uninterrupted. He will not necessarily live here, but wishes to stay from time to time for considerable periods. He wishes to inspect it tomorrow afternoon, and asks particularly that the place should be empty; that is to say, he will naturally bring the agent with him, but if you could arrange to leave the key…? About two o'clock if that's convenient. If he likes it he will purchase it at once, which means that the mortgage can be paid off immediately and since the price seems agreeable to him, there should be two or three hundred pounds for you, once everything outstanding is dealt with.'

'How nice,' said Sadie, and tried her best to sound delighted. Now that the crunch had come she was appalled at the idea of leaving not only the cottage but the village. She had lived there for twenty of her twenty-three years, and Chelcombe was her home. To earn her living she would have to go to a town, even a city, and she was going to hate it. Besides, there was Tom. She said forlornly: 'I must start looking for a job.'

Mr Banks eyed her thoughtfully. 'It might be a good idea if you put up in the village for a little while. You could go to Bridport on the bus—it goes twice a week, doesn't it? There is bound to be an employment agency there, it would be more satisfactory if you could obtain employment before you leave here.'

'I'll do that, Mr Banks. You've been awfully kind. I'm very grateful. I suppose—I suppose you don't know about the furniture?'

'No, and that at this stage can only be conjecture. If they wish to take over the house as it stands, then of course the buyer will pay for the contents, otherwise you will have to sell it, unless you can find unfurnished rooms. But if you intend going into domestic service then you could be expected to live at your place of work.' He frowned a little. 'Are you sure that there's nothing else that you can do?'

Sadie shook her head. 'I'm afraid not, but there must be plenty of housekeeping jobs, or mother's helps or something similar. In the country if I can, and with Tom, of course.'

Mr Banks heaved himself out of his chair. 'Well, my dear, I'm sure you will find just the work you are looking for. In the meanwhile, don't worry, things could have been much worse.'

With which doubtful comfort he went away.

The cottage already shone with polish and there wasn't a speck of dust to be seen. All the same, Sadie went all over it once more, making sure that it looked welcoming and cosy, and in the morning, she picked some of the chrysanthemums and eked them out with a great deal of evergreen from the hedge, and arranged a bowl here and a bowl there. She ate a hasty lunch then, made up the fire, put a guard before it, begged Tom to be a good quiet cat and not stir from his seat in the largest of the armchairs, put on her coat and headscarf, and let herself out into the bleak afternoon. She turned away from the village, for she had no wish to see whoever was coming, and walked briskly up the lane, winding its muddy way up to the crest of the hill. There was a magnificent view from the top in clear weather, but today the sad November afternoon was closing in already; in another hour it would be getting dark and even colder. She hoped that they would be gone by then; she would give them until four o'clock and then go back; if there were no lights on she would know that they had gone.

At the top of the hill she paused for breath, for

it was a steep climb and difficult going along the uneven lane, and then went on again, climbing over a stile and crossing a field to a five-barred gate with a cart track beyond it. The track was worse than the lane, but she splashed along in the muddy ruts, hardly noticing, her thoughts busy with her future. Presently she turned down a bridle path and followed it for a mile or more round the hill to come out at the top of the lane once more. By now it was almost dark; she could see the village lights twinkling below her and ten minutes downhill would bring her to the cottage. There was no light showing as she reached it. She went up the garden path quietly and tried the door. It was locked and she stooped to take the key from under the mat, where she had arranged for it to be left, and went inside.

It was warm indoors and she shed her coat and scarf and went into the sitting room to find the fire still burning nicely, and Tom still asleep. She went from room to room and found nothing had been disturbed, indeed she wondered if the man had come after all, and there was no way of finding out until the morning. She made tea and then got her supper; there was no point in planning her future until she knew what was to happen.

She knew that two days later when Charlie came whistling up the path to hand her a letter from Mr Banks. Mr Oliver Trentham wished to buy the cottage immediately. He waived a surveyor's report, raised no objection to the price and would take possession in the shortest possible time. Mr Banks added the information that after the mortgage had been paid and various fees, there would be just over three hundred pounds for her.

Sadie read it through twice and put it back in its envelope. So that was that, she wasn't sure how soon the shortest possible time would be, but she had better start packing up her own things. Mr Banks hadn't mentioned the furniture, which was annoying; she would have to write and find out and in the meantime go down to the village and see if Mrs Samways, who did bed and breakfast in the summer for those rare tourists who found their way to Chelcombe, would let her have a room until she had found herself a job. Tomorrow she would take the local bus into Bridport and see about a job.

She wrote her letter, posted it, answered Mrs Beamish's questions discreetly, and went along to see Mrs Samways. Yes, of course she could have a room and welcome, and Tom too, as long as she would be gone by Christmas. 'I've my brother Jim and his family coming over for two weeks,' she explained in her soft Dorset voice, 'and dear knows where I'm going to put 'em all.'

'Oh, I'll be gone by then,' Sadie assured her. 'Perhaps I won't want a room at all; I'm going to

Bridport tomorrow morning to see about a job. There's bound to be something.'

There wasn't. True, there were two house-keeper's jobs going, in large country houses, and not too far away, but they stipulated women over fifty and the agency lady, looking at Sadie's small thin person, and her gentle mouth, added her force-ful opinion that she simply wouldn't do.

There was a job for a lady gardener too, but there again, observed the lady with scorn, she was hardly suited, and she tut-tutted when Sadie confessed that she couldn't type or do shorthand, and hadn't got a Cordon Bleu certificate. 'What can you do?' she asked impatiently.

'Housework, and ironing and mending and just ordinary cooking—all the things a housewife does, I suppose. And I like children.'

'Well, there's nothing, dear. Come back next week and try again.' She added as Sadie stood up: 'You can always sign on, you know.'

Sadie thanked her. She would have to be des-perate to do that. Granny had belonged to a gen-eration that hadn't signed on, and she had drummed it into Sadie from an early age that it was something one didn't do unless one was on one's beam ends, and she wasn't that, not yet. She went back home and after her tea, composed an advertisement to put into the weekly local paper.

As it happened there was no need to send it. The next morning Charlie came plodding through the never-ending rain with another letter from Mr Banks. Sadie sat him down at the kitchen table and gave him a cup of tea while the letter burned a hole in her pocket.

'Bad luck about you having to leave,' observed Charlie. 'We'm all that put out. Pity it do be the wrong time of year for work, like.'

Sadie poured herself another cup and sat down opposite him. 'I hate to go, Charlie, I'm just hoping I'll find something to do not too far away.'

'Happen it's good news in your letter?'

'Well, no, Charlie, I don't think so. The cottage is sold—he'd have known that, of course—I expect it's something to do with that.'

He got up and opened the door on to the wind and the rain. 'Well, I'll be off. Be seeing you.'

She closed the door once he'd reached the gate and got on his bike to go back to the village, then she whipped the letter out and tore it open. It was brief and businesslike, but then Mr Banks was always that. The new owner of the cottage had enquired as to the possibility of finding a housekeeper for the cottage and he, Mr Banks, had lost no time in putting her name forward. She would live in and receive a salary to be agreed upon at a later date. He strongly advised her to accept the post, and would she let him know as soon as possible if she wished to take the job?

Sadie read the letter through several times, picked up the placid Tom and danced round the kitchen until she was out of breath. 'We're saved!' she told him. 'We're going to stay here, Tom...' She paused so suddenly that Tom let out a protesting mew. 'But only if we can both stay—I must be certain of that.' She put him down again, bundled into her mac and wellies and hurried down to the village.

Mrs Beamish wished her a good morning and in the same breath: 'Charlie popped his head in,' she observed, 'said you'd a letter from London again.' She eyed Sadie's face with interested curiosity. 'Good news, is it, love?'

It was nice to have someone to tell. Sadie poured the whole lot out and to the accompaniment of, 'He be a good man, surely,' and 'Well I never did, Miss Sadie, love,' she asked if she might use the telephone. The village had a phone box, erected by some unimaginative person a good half a mile from the village itself and for that reason seldom used.

Mrs Beamish not only lent the phone, she stayed close by so that she didn't miss a word of what was said, nodding her head at Sadie's 'Yes, Mr Banks, no, Mr Banks,' and then, 'but Bob the thatcher won't work in this weather: he'll have to wait until the spring.' She looked anxiously at Mrs Beamish, who nodded her head vigorously. 'No, it doesn't leak,' said Sadie, 'it looks as though it might, but I promise you it doesn't. And what about the furniture?'

She stood listening so intently that Mrs Beamish got a little impatient and coughed, then looked put out when Sadie said finally, 'All right, Mr Banks, and thank you very much.'

There were two more customers in the shop now, both listening hard. 'What about the furniture, Sadie?' one of them asked.

'Well, he wants it, most of it, that is, but he's bringing rugs and things like that—they're to be delivered some time during next week. Mr Banks says I'll have to be at home to put things straight and get in groceries and so on.'

'So he'll be here well before Christmas?' asked Mrs Beamish, her eyes sliding over her shelves of tins and packets. He might be a good customer.

'Yes, I expect so, but I don't know if he'll be here for Christmas. I suppose it's according to whether he has to work.'

'Well, love, we're that pleased—it'll bring a bit of life to the village, having a real writer here. I suppose he'll have a car, but where is he going to put it?'

'There's room for a garage if he opens the hedge

a bit further up the lane, and he can park on that bit of rough grass just opposite the gate,' said Sadie.

Everyone nodded and Mrs Beamish said: 'You just go into the sitting room, love, while I serve Mrs Cowley and Mrs Hedger, then we'll have a nice cup of tea together—we could make out a list of groceries you might want at the same time.'

And for the next few days Sadie had no time to brood. She missed Granny more than she could say, but life had to go on and as far as she could see it was going to go on very much as before. She had run the cottage and looked after her grandmother for two or three years: instead of an old lady there would be a middle-aged man. She had a vivid picture of him in her head—rather like Mr Banks only much more smartly dressed because presumably playwrights moved in the best circles. He wouldn't want to know about the running of the cottage, only expect his meals on time and well cooked, his shirts expertly ironed, the house cleaned and the bath water hot. Well, she could do all that, and she would be doing it in her own home too.

She took the bus to Bridport and bought herself two severe nylon overalls and a pair of serviceable felt slippers so that she wouldn't disturb him round the house and experimented with her hair—something severe, she decided, so that she would look mature and sensible, but her fine mouse coloured hair refused to do as she wished; the bun she screwed it into fell apart within an hour, and she was forced to tie it back with a ribbon as she always had done.

After a week, things began to arrive from a succession of vans making their way through the mud of the lane to the gate. Rugs, silky and fine and sombre-coloured, a large desk, a magnificent armchair, a crate of pictures, fishing rods and golf clubs. Sadie unpacked everything but the pictures and stowed them away. The dining room, which she and Granny had almost never used, would be his study, she imagined. She moved out the table and chairs and the old carpet, and laid one of the splendid ones which she had unwrapped with something like awe, and when Charlie came with the letters, she got him to help her move the desk into the centre of the room. She added a straightbacked armchair from the sitting room, a small sofa table from Granny's bedroom and the bedside lamp from her own room. It wasn't quite suitable, for it had a shade painted with pink roses, but it would be better than the old-fashioned overhead light in the centre of the room. It looked nice when she had finished, and she laid a fire ready in the small grate; there was nothing like a fire to give a welcome.

She rearranged the biggest bedroom too, laying another of the rugs and moving in a more comfortable chair. The rest of the furniture was old-fashioned but pleasant enough, although the wallpaper was old-fashioned and faded here and there. The sitting room she left more or less as it was, shabby but comfortable; she had put the dining room table at one end of it and put the new armchair close to the fireplace and moved out a smaller table and another chair and put them in her own room. By and large she was well satisfied with her efforts.

She had had one brief letter from Mr Banks, assuring her that all was going well; he would let her know the date of Mr Trentham's arrival as soon as possible. By then she had cleaned and polished, tidied the shed, chopped firewood and pored over the only cookery book in the house. It was to be hoped that Mr Trentham wasn't a man to hanker after mousseline of salmon or tournedos saut; Sadie comforted herself with the thought that if he was past his first youth, he would settle for simple fare. She made an excellent steak and kidney pudding and her pastry was feather-light.

It was two days later that she had another letter from Mr Banks, telling her that Mr Trentham proposed to take up residence in three days time. A cheque was enclosed—housekeeping money paid in advance so that she could stock up the larder; her salary and the remainder of the household expenses would be paid to her at a later date. He regretted that he was unable to say at what time of day Mr Trentham would arrive, but she should be prepared to serve a meal within a reasonable time of his arrival at the cottage. He added a warning that her employer was deeply involved in a television script and required the utmost quiet, qualifying this rather daunting statement with the hope that Sadie's troubles were now over and that she would make the most of her good fortune.

He didn't need to warn her about being quiet, thought Sadie rather crossly. There was no TV in the cottage simply because Granny had never been able to afford one; there was a radio, but she would keep that in her own room and she wasn't a noisy girl around the house. There was, in fact, nothing to be noisy with. Mr Trentham could write in the dining room with the door shut firmly upon him and not be disturbed by a sound.

That afternoon she went down to Mrs Beamish's shop with a list of groceries and spent a delightful half hour stocking up necessities to the satisfaction of herself and still more of Mrs Beamish. And the next morning she went into Bridport and cashed her cheque before purchasing several items Mrs Beamish didn't have, as well as visiting the butcher's and arranging for him to call twice a week. He delivered to Mrs Frobisher and the Manor House anyway, and

she assured him that it would be worth his while.
It was sitting in the bus on the way home that she
began to wonder about Christmas. It seemed un-
likely that Mr Trentham would want to stay at the
cottage, especially as he had children, in which case
she and Tom would spend it together, but Christmas
was still five weeks away and it was pointless to
worry about it.

She spent the evening storing away her purchases
and the next morning went to pay Mrs Beamish's
bill, ask William the milkman to let her have more
milk, and then tramped through the village to Mrs
Pike's Farm to order logs. Together with almost
everyone else in the village, she was in the habit of
wooding in the autumn and she had collected a useful pile of branches and sawn them ready for burning, but with two, perhaps three fires going, there
wouldn't be enough. And that done, she went home
and had her tea and then sat by the fire with Tom
on her lap, deciding what she would cook for Mr
Trentham's first meal.

She made a steak and kidney pudding after
breakfast the next morning because that couldn't
spoil if he arrived late in the day, and then peeled
potatoes and cleaned sprouts to go with it. For afters
she decided on Queen of Puddings, and since she
had time to spare she made a batch of scones and
fruit cake. With everything safely in the oven she

made a hasty meal of bread and cheese and coffee and flew up to her room to tidy herself. It was barely two o'clock, but he could arrive at any moment. She donned one of the new overalls, a shapeless garment which did nothing for her pretty figure, brushed her hair and tied it back, dabbed powder on her nose and put on lipstick sparingly; if she used too much she wouldn't look like a housekeeper.

The afternoon wore on into the early dark of a winter's evening. She made tea and ate a scone and had just tidied away her cup and saucer when she heard a car coming up the lane. She glanced at the clock—half past five; tea at once and supper about eight o'clock, perhaps a bit earlier, as he was probably cold and tired. She gave the fire in the sitting room a quick nervous poke and went to open the door.

Mr Trentham stepped inside and shut the door behind him. In silence he stood, staring down at her, a long lean man with thick dark hair, grey eyes and a face which any girl might dream about. He wasn't middle-aged or short, or stout; anyone less like Mr Banks Sadie had yet to meet. She stared back at him, conscious of a peculiar feeling creeping over her. She shook it off quickly and held out a hand. 'Good evening, Mr Trentham,' she said politely, 'I hope you had a good drive down. I'm Sadie Gillard, the housekeeper.'

He was smiling at her with lazy good humour, and she smiled back, relieved that he was so friendly, not at all what she had expected. Indeed, already the future was tinted with a faint rose colour. Thoughts went scudding through her head: she should have made a chocolate cake as well as the usual fruit one and got in beer. Mr Darling at the Bull and Judge would have known what to sell her...thank heaven she had made that steak and kidney pudding... She was brought down to earth by his voice, slow and deep, faintly amused.

'There seems to have been some mistake—I understood that there was to be a sensible country-woman.' His smile widened. 'I'm afraid you won't do at all.'

CHAPTER TWO

SHE FOUGHT DOWN instant panic. 'I am a sensible countrywoman,' she told him in a calm little voice, 'your housekeeper, and I can't think why I won't do, especially as you haven't eaten a meal here or slept in a bed or had your washing and ironing done yet.'

He had his head a little on one side, watching her, no longer smiling. 'You don't understand,' he told her quite gently. 'I'm looking for a quiet, experienced woman to run this cottage with perfection and no unnecessary noise. I write for a living and I have to have peace.'

'I'm as experienced as anyone will ever be. I've lived here in this cottage for twenty years, I know every creaking board and squeaking door and how to avoid them...'

His eyes narrowed. 'Of course, stupid of me— you're Mrs Gillard's granddaughter. To turn you out of your home would be decidedly unkind.' His faint smile came again. 'At least tonight. We'll discuss it in the morning.' He turned to the door again and opened it on to the chilly evening. 'I'll get my bags.'

When he came back with the first of them Sadie asked: 'Would you like tea, sir?'

'Yes, I would, and for God's sake don't call me sir!' He disappeared into the blackness again and she went to put the kettle on and butter the scones. She had laid a tray with Granny's best china and one of her old-fashioned traycloths and she carried it into the sitting room and put it on a small table by the fire. By the time he had brought in a considerable amount of luggage and taken off his sheepskin jacket, she had made the tea and carried it in.

'What about you?' he asked as he sat down, 'or have you already had yours?'

'Yes, thank you, I have. If you want more of anything will you call? I shall be in the kitchen.' At the door she paused. 'Would you like your supper at any particular time, Mr Trentham?'

He spread her home-made jam on a scone and took a bite. 'Did you make these?' he asked.

'Yes.'

'Wild strawberry jam,' he observed to no one in particular, 'I haven't tasted it since I was a boy. You made it?'

'Yes.' She tried again. 'Your supper, Mr Trentham?'

'Oh, any time,' he told her carelessly. 'I'll unpack a few things and get my books put away. Where have you put my desk?'

'In the other room. If you wouldn't mind having your meals in here, you could use the dining room to work in.'

He nodded. 'That sounds all right. Whose cat is that, staring at me from under the table?'

'Oh, that's Tom—he's mine. I did ask about him, and you said you wouldn't mind...'

'So I did.' He buttered another scone. 'Don't let me keep you from whatever you're doing.'

She went out closing the door soundlessly. The kitchen was warm and smelt deliciously of food. She put the custardy part of the Queen of Puddings into the oven and began to whip the egg whites. Her future was tumbling about her ears, but that was no reason to present him with a badly cooked meal. When she heard him go into the hall she opened the kitchen door to tell him: 'Your bedroom is the one on the right at the top of the stairs. Would you like any more tea, Mr Trentham?'

He paused, his arms full of books. 'No, thanks. It was the best tea I've had in years. In fact I don't normally have tea, I can see that I shall have to get into the habit again. Did you make that cake too?'

'Yes.' She went past him up the stairs and switched on the light in the bedroom and pulled the curtains. It looked very pleasant in a shabby kind of way but a bit chilly, she was glad she'd put hot water bottles in the bed.

'You can come in here and help,' he called as she went downstairs, and she spent the next half hour handing him books from the two big cases he had brought with him, while he arranged them on the bookshelves she had luckily cleared. He had a powerful desk lamp too and a typewriter, and a mass of papers and folders which he told her quite sharply to leave alone. Finally he said: 'That's enough for this evening.' He gave her his lazy smile again. 'Thanks for helping.'

He went outside again presently to the car parked in the lane and came back with a case of bottles which he arranged on the floor in a corner of the sitting room, an arrangement which Sadie didn't care for at all. There was a small table in one of the empty bedrooms; she would bring it down in the morning and put the bottles on it. She collected the tea tray and started to lay supper at one end of the table, and he asked for a glass.

Granny's corner cupboard was one of the nicest pieces of furniture in the cottage. Sadie opened its door now and invited him to take what he wanted. He chose a heavy crystal tumbler and held it up to the light.

'Very nice too—old—Waterford, I believe.'

'Yes, everything there is mostly Waterford, but

there are one or two glasses made by Caspar Wistar. My grandmother had them from her grandmother. I'm not sure how they came into the family.'

'They're rare and valuable.'

She closed the cupboard door carefully. 'I don't know if you bought them with the cottage. Mr Banks is going to send me a list...'

He had picked up a bottle of whisky and was pouring it. 'No, I haven't bought them, and if you think of selling them I should get a very reliable firm to value them first.'

'Sell them?' She looked at him quite blankly. 'But I couldn't do that!'

He shrugged his wide shoulders. 'No, probably you couldn't,' he agreed goodnaturedly. 'Something smells good,' he added.

'It will be ready in ten minutes,' she told him, and went back to the kitchen.

Washing up in the old-fashioned scullery later, Sadie wondered what her chances of staying were. Undoubtedly, when they had met, Mr Trentham had made up his mind instantly that she wouldn't do, but now, since making inroads into the splendid supper she had put before him, she had seen his eyes, thoughtful and a little doubtful, resting upon her as she had cleared the table. She hadn't said a word, just taken in the coffee and put it silently on the table by the fire, then taken herself off to the kitchen, where she and Tom demolished the rest of the steak and kidney pudding and the afters before setting the kitchen to rights again. It was bedtime before she had finished. She refilled the hot water bottle, switched on the bedside light and went downstairs again to tap on the sitting room door and go in.

'There's plenty of hot water if you would like a bath,' she told him, 'and it will be warm enough by eight o'clock in the morning if you'd prefer one then.'

He looked up from the book he was reading. 'Oh, the morning, I think.'

'If you'd put the guard in front of the fire?' she suggested. 'I hope you'll sleep well, Mr Trentham.'

He smiled at her. 'No doubt of that,' he assured her. 'I've been sitting here listening for the proverbial pin to drop. I'd forgotten just how quiet it can be in the country.'

She nodded. 'Yes. Goodnight, Mr Trentham.'

'Goodnight, Sadie.'

She went up the narrow stairs, Tom plodding behind her to climb on to her bed and make himself comfortable while she had a bath and got ready for the night. She was almost asleep when she heard Mr Trentham come upstairs. He came with careful stealth, trying to be quiet, but he was a big man and probably not used to considering others all that much. He was nice, though, she thought sleepily, used to doing as he pleased, no doubt, but then according to Charlie, who read the *TV Times* and watched the box whenever he had a moment to spare, he was an important man in his own particular field. She heard his door on the other side of the landing close quietly and then silence, broken by a subdued bellow of laughter.

She was too tired to wonder about that.

She was up before seven o'clock, creeping downstairs to clear out the ashes and light the fires in both rooms as well as the boiler and then to get dressed before going down to the kitchen to cook the breakfast—porridge and eggs and bacon and toast. By the time Mr Trentham got down the table was laid and the fire was burning brightly. She wished him a sedate good morning and added: 'Tea or coffee?'

'Coffee, please. God, I haven't had a night like that in years!'

There seemed no answer to that. Sadie retired to the kitchen, made the coffee and took it in with a bowl of porridge.

'I never eat the stuff,' declared Mr Trentham, and then at the sight of her downcast face: 'Oh, all right, I'll try it.'

She had the satisfaction of seeing a bowl scraped clean when she took in the eggs and bacon. He

demolished those too before polishing off the toast
and marmalade.

'It goes without saying that you made the marmalade as well,' he observed as she cleared the table.

'Well, yes, of course. Everyone does.' She gave
him a brief smile and went back to the kitchen,
where she ate her breakfast with Tom for company
until Charlie interrupted her with a pile of letters.

'Brought a bit o' custom to the village,' he volunteered cheerfully. 'That's a posh car outside, all
right.'

Sadie gobbled up the last of her bacon, offered
a mug of tea and took the letters. Mr Trentham
wasn't in the sitting room and she could hear the
typewriter going without pause. She didn't fancy
disturbing him, not after all his remarks about peace
and quiet, but she saw no way out of it. She tapped
on the door and getting no answer, went in, laid the
post down on the edge of the desk and went out
again. She rather doubted if he had seen her.

She whisked round the cottage, not finding much
to do, for everything had been so scrubbed and polished it had had no time to get even a thin film of
dust. And then, since the typewriter was still being
pounded without pause, she went silently in with
coffee. Without looking up, Mr Trentham said:
'Open the post for me, Sadie, will you? Do it here.'

She thought of her own coffee cooling in the kitchen and picked up a paper knife on the desk. There were nine letters. Three of them were in handwriting and began Dear Oliver, and she laid them on top of the others—bills and what appeared to be business letters. Having done so she made silently for the door, to be stopped by Mr Trentham's voice.

'Where's your coffee?'

'In the kitchen.' She put a hand on the door knob.

'Fetch it and come back here, I want to have a talk with you.' He sounded so noncommittal that she guessed that he was going to tell her that she must go. And where to? she asked herself, rejoining him, her tranquil face showing nothing of the panic she was in.

'Mr Banks was quite right,' he began. 'He described you as a sensible countrywoman, and it seems to me you are. What my mother would have called an old head on young shoulders…I think we may suit each other very well, Sadie, but several adjustments must be made. We'll take our meals together—it's ridiculous that you should eat in the kitchen of your own home. You will share the sitting room as you wish, all I ask is that I should be left to myself in this room. You will refrain from lugging logs and coals into the house, I'll do that each morning or if you prefer, each night. And you're not to wear that depressing overall. We'll go to Bridport and purchase something more in keeping with your age. What is your age, by the way?'

'I'm twenty-three.'

He nodded. 'There are things to be done to the cottage. It needs a new thatch, I need a garage; a shower room would be useful. I've already arranged for a telephone to be installed, and someone should be here later today to install television.' He searched in his pockets and pulled out a cheque book. 'Here's housekeeping money until the end of the month, after that you'll be paid it on the first of each month.' He started on another cheque. 'And here's a week's salary in advance. You'll get a month's money at the same time as the housekeeping.'

He pushed the cheques towards her and she picked them up in a daze.

'All that, just for housekeeping?' she wanted to know.

'I like good food—good plain food, well cooked. I abhor things in tins and packets and frozen peas.'

'Well, there isn't a freezer,' she explained, 'and I hardly ever buy things in tins because they're too expensive.'

He smiled at her and her heart lurched. 'Splendid!' He gave her an encouraging nod and thought how beautiful her eyes were in her plain little face.

There was nothing about her to distract him from his work. 'The tradespeople call?' he wanted to know.

'Yes, and Mrs Beamish has almost all the groceries we need. I get eggs from someone in the village and I've ordered some more logs from a farm near by—they've cut down some trees and we can buy the awkward logs that won't sell easily.'

'Yes.' He sounded a little impatient and she got up, put the coffee cups on the tray.

'I'll be in the garden if you want me for anything, Mr Trentham. What would you like for lunch?'

He had picked up a sheaf of papers and was frowning over them. 'Oh, anything—we'll eat this evening.'

There was plenty of soup left over from the previous day and a mackerel pâté she had made; toast wouldn't take an instant and she could make a Welsh rarebit in no time at all. She got into her wellies and the old mac and went into the garden to cut a cabbage.

At one o'clock precisely she put her head round the door to say that lunch was about to be put on the table, and found him sitting back with a drink in his hand. He got up and followed her into the kitchen and watched while she ladled the soup and then carried the tray for her.

Beyond stating that he seldom stopped for a meal

when he was working, he had nothing to say, but
Sadie noticed that every drop of soup was eaten and
when she replaced that with Welsh rarebit, he ate
that too—moreover, the pâté followed it. It was obvious to her that he hadn't been eating properly.
Well, the housekeeping money he had given her
was more than enough to buy the best of everything.

She put his coffee on the table by the fire and
went away to wash up. He had insisted that she
should take her meals with him, but that didn't
mean that she was to bear him company at any
other time. She tidied the kitchen, told him that she
would be going out for an hour and would be back
in good time to get his tea, and wrapped up in her
old coat, walked down to the village. Mr Trentham
wanted papers to be delivered each morning and
they needed to be ordered. She paused outside the
gate to look at the car: an Aston Martin Volante. It
looked a nice car, she considered, and beautifully
upholstered inside, and she remembered vaguely
that it was expensive. It was a shame to keep it out
in the cold and damp of November, the sooner Mr
Trentham had a garage built the better.

The newspapers were ordered from Mrs Beamish
and that entailed a brief gossip about the cottage's
owner. Everyone in the village seemed to have seen
him driving through and there was a good deal of

speculation about him. Sadie was forced to admit
that she knew next to nothing about him and wasn't
likely to.

When she got back there was a van parked behind the car and a man on the roof fixing an aerial
and another man inside installing the TV. Sadie
went into the kitchen where Tom was drowsing by
the stove, laid a tray for tea and made two mugs
and carried them out to the men. Judging by the
impatient voice coming from the dining room, Mr
Trentham was being disturbed in his work and
wasn't best pleased. She smoothed them down,
poured them second mugs and gave them a pound
from the housekeeping. When they had gone Mr
Trentham summoned her into the dining room,
where he was sitting at his desk; there were
screwed-up balls of paper all over the floor and he
looked in a bad temper. 'How can I work with all
that noise?' he demanded of her.

'You arranged for the television to be brought,'
she reminded him mildly. 'They've finished and
gone, and since you're not working for the moment
I'll make the tea.'

The ill humour left his face and he smiled at her.
'You're not at all like a housekeeper—I have one
at my Highgate home and she spends her days running away from me.'

'Whatever for?' asked Sadie matter-of-factly. 'Would you like your tea on a tray here?'

'No, I would not. I'll have it with you.'

And later over his second cup of tea and third slice of cake, he observed: 'I shall get fat.'

'You can always go for a walk,' she suggested diffidently. 'The countryside is pretty and once you're out you don't notice the weather.'

'I've too much work to do.' He sounded impatient again, so she held her tongue and when he had finished, cleared away with no noise at all, and presently, in the kitchen peeling potatoes, she heard the typewriter once more.

The next morning he drove her into Bridport and much to her astonishment stalked into the biggest dress shop there and stood over her while she chose some overalls. Money, it seemed, was no object. The cheaper ones she picked out were cast aside and she was told with what she recognised as deceptive mildness to get something pretty. Taking care not to look at the price tickets, she chose three smocks in cheerful coloured linen and watched him pay for them without so much as a twitch of an eyebrow.

It was two days later when the washing machine arrived, and she had barely got over her delighted surprise at that when someone came to install the telephone with an extension in the dining room so that Mr Trentham could use it without having to move from his desk. It was becoming increasingly apparent to her that his work was very important to him; he made desultory conversation during their meals together and he regarded her with a kind of lazy good humour, but for the rest she was a cog in smooth-running machinery which engineered his comfort.

At the end of a week she knew nothing more about him and he in his turn evinced no interest whatever in herself. On Sunday she had been considerably surprised when he had accompanied her to church and after the service allowed her to introduce him to Mr Frobisher, who in turn introduced him to the Durrants from the Manor House. They bore him off for drinks, and Mrs Durrant bestowed a kindly nod upon Sadie as they went. She hadn't meant to be patronising, Sadie told herself as she went back to the cottage. She got the lunch ready and sat down to wait. After an hour Mrs Durrant rang up to say that Mr Trentham was staying there for lunch, so Sadie drank her coffee and made a scrambled egg on toast for herself, fed Tom and got into her old coat, tied a scarf round her hair and went for a walk.

It had turned much colder and the rain had stopped at last. She crunched over the frosty ground, finding plenty to think about. She had been paid a month's salary the evening before and she intended to spend most of it on clothes. She climbed the hill briskly, her head full of tweed coats, pleated skirts, slacks and woolly jumpers. She wouldn't be able to get them all at once, of course, and after those would come shoes and undies and at least one pretty dress. She had no idea when she would wear it, but it would be nice to have it hanging in the wardrobe. Besides, there was Christmas. She hadn't been able to accept any invitations for the last two Christmases because of Granny being an invalid, but perhaps this year she would be free for at least part of the holiday. She frowned as she thought that possibly Mr Trentham would go home to his other house for Christmas and New Year too; he'd want to be with his family and he must have loads of friends in London, in which case she would be on her own.

There was a biting wind blowing when she reached the top of the hill, and she turned and walked back again in the gathering dusk. There were no lights on, the cottage was in darkness; Mr Trentham would be staying at the Manor for tea. Sadie let herself in quietly, took off her coat and went into the kitchen to put on the kettle. Mr Trentham was asleep in the comfortable shabby old chair by the stove with Tom on his knee. He opened his eyes when she switched on the light and said at once: 'Where have you been? I wanted to talk to you and you weren't here.'

'I go for a walk every afternoon,' she reminded him. 'I thought you might be staying at the Durrants' for tea. It's almost tea time, I'll get it now if you would like me to.'

He nodded. 'And can we have it here?'

She didn't show her surprise. 'Yes, of course.' She put a cloth on the table and fetched the chocolate cake she had made the day before and began to cut bread and butter, a plateful thinly sliced and arranged neatly.

'You'd better go into Bridport and buy yourself some clothes,' said Mr Trentham suddenly. 'Better still, I'll drive you to a town where there are more shops. Let's see—how about Bath?'

Sadie warmed the teapot. 'That would be heavenly, but you don't need to drive me there, Mr Trentham, I can get a bus to Taunton or Dorchester.'

'I have a fancy to go to Bath, Sadie. When did you last buy clothes?'

She blushed. 'Well, not for quite a long while, you see, Granny couldn't go out, so there wasn't any need...'

'Nor any money,' he finished blandly. 'I must buy the girls Christmas presents and I shall need your advice.'

'How old are they?'

'Five and seven years old—Anna and Julie. They have a governess, Miss Murch. Could you cope with the three of them over Christmas?'

Sadie didn't stop to think about it. 'Yes, of course. Only you'll need to buy another bed— would the little girls mind sleeping in the same room?'

'I imagine not, they share a room at Highgate. What else shall we need?'

She poured the tea and offered him the plate of bread and butter. 'That's blackcurrant jam,' she told him. 'Well, a Christmas tree and fairy lights and decorations and paper chains.' She was so absorbed that she didn't see the amusement on his face. 'A turkey and all the things that go with it—I'll be making the puddings myself, and a cake, of course, and crackers and mince pies and sausage rolls...' She glanced at him. 'The children will expect all that.'

'Will they? I was in America last Christmas; I believe Miss Murch took them to a hotel.' He smiled a little and she saw the mockery there. 'Don't look so shocked, Sadie, I suspect that you're a little out of date.'

She shook her head. 'You can't be out of date over Christmas. Even when there's not much money it can still be magic...'

He passed her the cake and took a slice himself. 'You're so sure, aren't you? Shall we give it a whirl, then? Buy what you want and leave the bills to me.'

'Yes, Mr Trentham—only you are sure, aren't you? The country is very quiet—I mean, in the town—London—there's always so much to do, I imagine, and there's nothing here. The Carol Service, and a party for the children and perhaps a few friends coming in.'

'I'm quite sure, Sadie, and it will be something quite different for the children. Now when shall we go to Bath?'

'Well, I'd like to get the washing done tomorrow…we could go on Tuesday. Do you want to buy the girls' presents then?'

'Certainly, though I have no idea what to get—I believe they have everything.'

She began to clear away the tea things. 'Do they like dolls?'

'Yes, I'm sure they do.' He sounded impatient and when he got out of the chair she said quietly: 'Supper will be about half past seven, Mr Trentham, if that suits you?'

He gave a grunting reply and a minute later she heard the typewriter. He was, she decided, a glutton for work.

It was cold and bright and frosty on Tuesday, and

leaving Tom in charge curled up by the fire, they set out directly after breakfast. Sadie had on her best coat, bought several years earlier more with an eye to its warmth and durability than its fashion. She wore her hat too, a plain felt of the same mouse brown as the coat. Mr Trentham glanced at her and then away again quickly. The women he took out were smart, exquisitely turned out and very expensive. There was only one word for Sadie and that was dowdy. He felt suddenly very sorry for her, and then, taking another quick glance at her happy young face, realised that his pity was quite wasted.

They parked the car in the multi-storey car park and walked the short distance to the centre of the city, but before Sadie was allowed to look at shop windows they had coffee in an olde-worlde coffee shop near the Abbey, and only when they had done that did they start their shopping.

Sadie had supposed that he would arrange to meet her for lunch and go off on his own, but he showed no sign of doing this, instead he led the way towards Milsom Street shopping precinct where all the better shops were. 'Blue or green,' he told her, examining the models in the windows, 'and don't buy a hat, get a beret. How much money have you?'

She didn't mind him being so dictatorial, it was like being taken out by an elder brother, she supposed. 'Well, the salary you gave me, and I've some money in the bank…'

'How much?'

'Mr Banks isn't quite sure, but at least two hundred pounds.' She looked at him enquiringly. Not a muscle of his face moved, as he said gravely:

'I should think you could safely spend half of that as well as your salary—you'll only need a little money for odds and ends, won't you?'

'Well, I must get one or two Christmas presents.'

'Probably the amount Mr Banks sends you will be more than he estimates.'

'You think so? Then I'll spend half of it.' Then her face clouded. 'Only I haven't got it yet.'

'I'll let you have a hundred pounds and you can repay me when you get it.'

She hesitated. 'You don't mind?'

'Not in the least. It would be highly inconvenient if I had to spend another day shopping.' He added with the lazy good humour she was beginning to recognise: 'So let's enjoy ourselves today.'

It took her a little while to get started; she had never had so much money to spend before in her life and she was afraid to break into the wad of notes in her purse. They went from one shop to the next, and if Mr Trentham was bored he never said so. Sadie settled finally on a green tweed coat and a matching skirt with a beret to match it and, since they hadn't cost a great deal, a sapphire blue wool dress, very simply cut. By then it was time for lunch. He took her to a restaurant called The Laden Table in George Street. It was fairly small but fashionable and Sadie wished with all her heart that she was wearing the new outfit, but she forgot that presently, made very much at her ease by Mr Trentham, who when he chose to exert himself could be an amusing companion. Besides, the food was delicious and the glass of sherry he offered her before they started their meal went to her head so that she forgot that she was by far the shabbiest woman in the room.

She spent the afternoon mostly by herself. Now that Mr Trentham had guided her away from the dreary colours which did nothing for her, he felt that he could safely leave her. 'Get a pretty blouse or two,' he suggested casually, 'and a couple of sweaters—and no brown, mind. I'll be at the coffee house at four o'clock, and mind you don't keep me waiting.'

So she spent a long time in Marks and Spencer, and came out loaded, not only with the blouses and sweaters but with a pink quilted dressing gown and slippers and a pile of undies. There was precious little money left in her purse, but she didn't care; she had all the things she had wanted most and she was content.

She got to the coffee house with a minute to spare and found him already there. She turned a radiant face to his and he took her parcels. 'I've bought everything I ever wanted,' she told him breathlessly, 'well, almost everything. It's been a lovely day.'

Over tea she asked him: 'Did you get the presents for your little girls?'

He nodded. 'I took your advice and got those workbaskets you liked. It seems a funny present for a little girl…'

'No, it's not; they like doing things, you know, and it isn't like asking for a needle and cotton from a grown-up, everything in the basket's theirs.'

'I'll take your word for it. If you've finished your tea we'd better go, Tom will be in despair.'

Sadie sat beside him in the car, enjoying the speed and his good driving. It was a cold dark evening now, but the car was warm and very comfortable, and since he didn't want to talk, she thought about her new clothes and imagined herself wearing them. Mrs Durrant would no longer be able to look down her beaky nose at her on Sundays, and at Christmas she would wear the blue dress.

At the cottage, the car unloaded and the parcels on the kitchen table, Mr Trentham said briefly: 'I'd like bacon and eggs for my supper,' and stalked away to the dining room and presently she heard the clink of bottle and glass and sighed. He drank a little too much, she considered. To counteract the whisky, she would give him cocoa with his supper.

She fed Tom, made up the fire and went to take off her things. Unwrapping the parcels would have to come later; first Mr Trentham must have his eggs and bacon.

She set the table in the sitting room and called him when she had carried their meal in. He came at once and sat down without speaking. Only when he took a drink from his cup he put it down with a thump and a furious: 'What the hell's this I'm drinking?'

'Cocoa,' said Sadie mildly. Even in such a short time, she had got used to his sudden spurts of temper and took no notice of them.

Just for a moment she thought that he was going to fling it at her across the table. Instead he burst out laughing. 'I haven't had cocoa since I was a small boy.' He stared at her for a long moment. 'Now I'm a middle-aged man. How old do you think I am, Sadie?'

She was too honest to pretend that she hadn't thought about it. 'Well, it's hard to say,' she said carefully. 'When you're pleased about something you look about thirty-five.'

'And when I'm not pleased?'

'Oh, older, of course.' She smiled at him. 'Does it matter?'

'I'm forty next birthday,' he told her briefly. 'Does that seem very old to you?'

She shook her head. 'No, it's not even middle-aged. Besides, you've got your little daughters to keep you young.'

'So I have.' He sounded bitter and she wondered why, suddenly curious to know more about him. It was strange, the two of them living in the same house and knowing nothing about each other. She reminded herself that she worked for him, her life was so utterly different from what she imagined his to be when he wasn't living at the cottage. Presumably he would finish whatever he was working on that so engrossed him, and tire of the peace and quiet and go back to London.

He went back to the dining room when he'd finished his supper, calling a careless goodnight as he went, and presently Sadie went up to bed. She tried on all the new clothes before she turned out the light. They still looked marvellous, but for some reason the first excitement at wearing them had gone. There was, after all, no one to notice them, least of all Mr Trentham.

CHAPTER THREE

SADIE SAW very little of Mr Trentham for the next two or three days. He appeared for his meals and ate them with evident enjoyment, but for the greater part of the day he was shut in the dining room with his typewriter and when he did emerge it was to put on his sheepskin jacket and go for a walk. On the fourth morning, however, he drove off in his car, saying that he wouldn't be in for lunch, but hoped to be back for tea. Which gave Sadie a chance to rush through the cottage, making as much noise as she liked, polishing furniture and hoovering floors and cleaning windows. It took her all the morning, and after a quick lunch she sat down to write a list of all the things she would need to buy for Christmas. Mr Trentham had said spare no expense, and although she very much doubted if he would keep his plan to spend Christmas at the cottage, she would have to make all the preparations just the same.

Mr Trentham didn't come back for tea; nor did he come back for dinner. Sadie waited until after nine o'clock and when he didn't come, she ate some of the casserole she had made, and put the rest on one side to be warmed up at a minute's notice. At eleven o'clock she went to bed. It was silly to worry about him; he was a splendid driver, and a man of forty should be able to look after himself. It took her quite a time to get to sleep.

He turned up at nine o'clock the next morning, after she had eaten her own breakfast and got the fires going.

'I'd like my breakfast.' He had flung open the dining room door and was halfway into the room, without saying good morning or hullo. Now he paused to say testily: 'Well, why are you looking so disapproving?'

He was coldly, bleakly angry, but Sadie wouldn't admit even to herself that she was even faintly scared. 'You went away yesterday morning, Mr Trentham, and said that you expected to be back for tea. If you'd phoned I wouldn't have cooked supper...'

He said in an amused, mocking voice which she found worse than anger: 'Since when must I keep my housekeeper informed of my comings and goings?' He added: 'I don't pay you to be nosey.'

Sadie blushed so hotly that she could feel the whole of her face burning. All the same, she stood her ground. She said with great dignity: 'I was not being nosey...' She had intended to say a good deal more but altered it to, 'I'll get your breakfast at once.'

She was a gentle girl, not given to rages, but she seethed as she cooked bacon and eggs, mushrooms and crisps of fried bread; made coffee and toast. When it was done, she tapped on the dining room door, carried the tray through to the sitting room and went upstairs to her own room, where she sat down at the little table under the window which did duty as a desk, and in a neat hand wrote out her notice, pointing out in the politest way possible that she would be prepared to go at once if he wanted her to, otherwise she would work out her remaining weeks. There was, she advised him, an excellent agency in Bridport where she felt sure he would get someone to suit him in a very short time.

She addressed an envelope, stuck it down and once downstairs, put it on his desk before going back to the kitchen. Domestic upheavals or not, meals had to be got ready, and she had a tasty minestrone soup already simmering; it had taken her quite a time to prepare, and it was as different from the tinned variety as chalk from cheese. She was grinding a touch more pepper into its delicate aroma when the door burst open and Mr Trentham came charging in waving her notice.

'What the hell do you mean by this?' he demanded savagely.

Sadie put the pepper mill down and replaced the saucepan lid. 'Well, just what I said—wasn't it clear enough? I've never written one before, so I wasn't sure…'

'And don't you ever dare to write one again,' he warned her. 'Of all the silly female nonsense, just because I happened to be mildly touchy!'

She stood in front of him, small and thin and even in her gay smock only slightly pretty, but she was quite unruffled now only though a little pale. 'I am not a silly female,' she pointed out with calm, 'and if that's what you're like when you're mildly touchy then I shan't bother with writing my notice if you have an attack of real touchiness, I shall take Tom and go.' She prevented herself just in time from adding, 'So there!'

His great roar of laughter was disconcerting. It was just as disconcerting when he said gravely: 'If I apologise, will you stay, Sadie? You really are a splendid housekeeper, and if you can ignore my ill temper and my tiresome ways, I would be grateful if you will stay. You're like a mouse around the place and your cooking is out of this world.' He smiled with such charm that she found herself smiling back. He held out a hand. 'Shake on it—I'll promise not to lose my temper unless I'm absolutely driven to it.' And when they had solemnly shaken hands: 'Something smells delicious—is it lunch?' His elegant nose flared as he sniffed.

'Only soup, and it's for lunch.' She spoke in a matter-of-fact voice. 'Would you like your coffee now?'

'Please.' He rarely said please and she blinked her long lashes. 'And I want to talk to you about Christmas.'

'I'll be ten minutes, Mr Trentham.'

But he didn't mention Christmas to start with. 'I went to a conference,' he told her. 'I'm half way through a script for a series—short stories really, linked together by one theme, love. The producer couldn't see eye to eye with me about it,' his lip curled. 'The fellow could only see love in terms of bedroom scenes, but there's more to it than that—there must be, because some people have been lucky enough to find it. I've persuaded him to change his mind, but it left me...mildly touchy.'

She gave him a thoughtful look. 'Are you very famous?'

His brows rose. 'I could be falsely modest and say no, but I'll be honest and say that for the time being at least, yes, I'm famous among my kind.'

He passed his cup for more coffee. 'And what do you think about love, Sadie?'

'Me? Well, I don't know, when I was at school

I had crushes on tennis players and film actors, but I don't think I've been in love with anyone.'

Mr Trentham nodded. 'Well, it's for people like you I'm writing this series.'

'I expect I'll enjoy it, then.'

'You're free to give me an honest criticism when you see it. And now about Christmas. I'm going to fetch the children down next week—Miss Murch will come too, of course. They'll be here for about three weeks. Will you be able to manage? I'll get extra help in if you need it.'

'Oh, but why should I? Miss Murch will be here to look after Anna and Julie, won't she? And it's as easy to cook for five as it is for two, especially when I don't have to be economical.'

'Get all you need to make a good Christmas for the children. I shall be here for Christmas Day, but I've a number of invitations; I daresay I shall be away for a good deal of the time. Most of my friends live in London and there's a good deal of merry-making planned.'

Sadie felt a pang of disappointment. 'Yes, of course,' she agreed cheerfully, 'but there'll be plenty for the girls to do. Does Miss Murch like the country?'

'I haven't the least idea.' He was suddenly bored with it all and with a muttered excuse, went back to his typewriter.

Sadie went down to the village the next morning and gave Mrs Beamish an order to make that lady's eyes sparkle. 'My word,' she exclaimed, 'wouldn't your granny have been pleased, spending all that money on extras!'

And Sadie agreed, hiding a sorrow for the old lady because she knew that her grandmother would have disliked any sign of weakness. She unpacked the groceries Mrs Beamish's schoolboy son brought up to the cottage after lunch and Mr Trentham, coming into the kitchen for a slice of cake to fill the gap between lunch and tea, demanded to know if she had all she wanted.

'No,' said Sadie, 'if you don't mind, I'll take the bus into Bridport tomorrow and get the things I can't get here. Crackers, almonds, raisins and sweets, and give an order to the butcher—they like to know in plenty of time if you want a turkey, you know.'

'No, I didn't know. It seems my education has been sadly neglected in the domestic field.' He took a second slice of cake. 'I'll drive you in.'

'I might be ages.'

'I've some shopping to do too. But why don't we go to Dorchester? Aren't there more shops there?'

'I don't suppose there are many more, but there is a Marks and Spencer.'

'Good, we'll go directly after breakfast.'

It was a raw morning when they set out, with a freezing mist shrouding the high ground at Askerswell so that Mr Trentham had to slow down to a mere forty miles an hour. Sadie could feel his impatience mounting and said soothingly: 'It clears up once we get off the dual carriageway.'

She sat back, conning her shopping list, feeling elegant in her new coat and beret. If there was time she would buy some gloves and perhaps a pair of shoes. And presents for the little girls and of course, Miss Murch. She hoped she was young and that they would get on together; it would be nice to have someone of her own age at the cottage.

They had coffee before he left her to do the shopping, saying that he had some to do for himself, and he would meet her at one o'clock exactly at the King's Arms in High East Street. There was a splendidly old-fashioned grocers close to the hotel where Sadie knew that she would be able to get all the things she needed, she could go there last of all and have time to look for presents at her leisure. Handkerchiefs for Miss Murch, she decided; expensive hand-embroidered ones, and more difficult to find, two small dolls to be dressed in clothes she would make herself.

And something for Mr Trentham. What, she wondered, would be a suitable gift from a housekeeper to her employer? She found a book and old print shop and after a good deal of browsing found a small eighteenth-century map of Dorset, nicely framed. It was rather more than she had intended to pay, but the shoes could wait until her next pay day.

But as luck would have it, she found a pair of gloves which didn't cost anything like the money she had expected to pay, and in one of the shoe shops there was a special pre-Christmas offer of leather boots at a price she could just afford. She had her well polished, worthy shoes packed and wore the new boots and positively skimmed up South Street and into High East Street. She had half an hour before she was to meet Mr Trentham; just sufficient time in which to buy the things on her list.

They had everything—dried fruits and nuts, the finest tea, the best coffee, an assortment of biscuits to make her mouth water, boxes of crackers, cheeses, things in tins she had never bought before. She only hoped there would be enough money in the wad of notes Mr Trentham had given her.

There was. She paid and then stood looking at the cardboard box which had been neatly packed with her goodies. She already had a shopping basket crammed full besides her shoes; perhaps she could leave it there and they could pick it up after lunch. She was debating the point when Mr Trentham's distinguished head was thrust through the door.

'I've brought the car round to the hotel car park,' he told her, 'if there's any shopping...' His eye fell on the overflowing box on the counter. 'Good lord, have you bought all that?'

'I daresay it looks a lot, but there's nothing there we don't actually need.' She beamed a goodbye to the elderly man who had served her with such patience and gathered up her parcels, then watched while Mr Trentham heaved the box off the counter. With it safely stowed in the boot she gave a sigh of relief. 'How very lucky that the hotel should be right next door to the grocers,' she observed, 'and such a heavenly shop—they offer you a chair, you know, and call you madam.'

'They'd better not call me madam,' said Mr Trentham tartly. He slammed down the lid of the boot and locked it. 'Lunch—I'm famished!'

They ate roast beef and everything which went with it, and he declared that it wasn't a patch on her cooking, which pleased Sadie mightily and probably accounted for the pink in her cheeks, although the claret he had given her to drink might have been the cause of that. She ate the sherry trifle with uncritical appetite while Mr Trentham contented himself with a morsel of cheese, and then they went back to the car. As they got into it she said on a breath of excitement: 'It's three weeks to Christmas!'

He gave her a lazy mocking look. 'You're nothing but a child,' he observed, and then frowned and she wondered why.

'You don't like Christmas?' she asked, unaware that the frown had nothing to do with that at all.

They were crawling up High West Street in a queue of traffic. 'It's become a commercial holiday, I seem to have lost the real Christmas years ago.'

'You'll find it again in Chelcombe,' declared Sadie. 'I think...'

'And now hush, I want to think,' he told her brusquely.

She was getting used to his sudden fits of impatience and supposed he was working out a difficult bit of script, and anyway, she had plenty to think about herself—never mind what Mr Trentham thought about Christmas, his small daughters should have the very best one Sadie could contrive for them. She got out her notebook and began to write down the ingredients for the pudding. After a while Mr Trentham demanded: 'What are you writing?'

'The pudding.'

'Oh, God,' said Mr Trentham, and put his foot down on the accelerator so that she had to give up.

They were back in the cottage well before teatime and she was a little surprised when he declared his intention of going down to the village. 'Tea at the usual time?' she wanted to know.

'Oh, have yours if I'm not back by half past four,' he almost growled at her, so that she wondered what she'd done now.

She forgot about him almost at once; all the groceries had to be unpacked and stowed away and the presents borne upstairs to be packed up in coloured paper. Later on, when she had time, she would cut out the dolls' clothes and make them up. She tidied everything away, feeling happy.

She might not have felt so happy if she had known where Mr Trentham was—at the Vicarage, in Mr Frobisher's study, talking about her.

'I have only just realised,' said Mr Trentham snappily, 'that the village might consider Sadie's situation as—er—dubious. In London the permissive society wouldn't lift so much as an eyebrow over it, but here in Chelcombe it's possible that they look askance at her sharing the cottage with me. She's my housekeeper and nothing more, of that I can assure you, but I wouldn't wish anyone to speak ill of her; she's a splendid worker and a first class cook and runs the place smoothly. That's all I asked and hoped for.'

Mr Frobisher nodded, his balding head on one side. 'I appreciate your concern, but I can assure you that it's unnecessary. We've all known Sadie since she was a very small girl; her grandmother, an excellent woman, brought her up strictly and according to her own standards, which I must admit hadn't moved with the times. Sadie is in a consequence, a little straitlaced. I feel this to be a pity but that is merely my opinion, you understand. As for the rest of the village, in their eyes you're a widower with children, which sets you in a class apart and in need of all possible assistance. That you're a successful man cuts very little ice. You're liked, did you know that, because you've been the means of giving Sadie a livelihood and the blessing of living in her own home. You need have no fears as to Sadie's reputation, Mr Trentham, indeed she has earned added respect because she has a trustworthy, well paid position.' He smiled suddenly. 'Besides, you've brought custom to the village, you know; and I hear you're to spend Christmas here, and your little daughters, an excuse for the local residents to hold dinner parties and so forth.'

Mr Trentham looked surprised. 'Oh, delightful, we shall look forward to that.' He stood up, preparing to go, but Mrs Frobisher, timing it nicely, put her head round the door with an invitation to stay to tea. It was dark by the time he let himself into the cottage, to find Sadie at the kitchen table making dumplings for the stew. They had had a good lunch, but she had never known Mr Trentham refuse food yet. She looked up as he went into the kitchen and offered to make tea, but he refused, told her that he didn't want his supper until at least eight o'clock, and went into the dining room and began pounding the typewriter; making up for lost time, she supposed.

Sadie had never known a week fly past so fast; what with the puddings to make, the cakes to bake, the stowing of a great many bottles delivered for Mr Trentham, the preparing of the bedrooms for the children and Miss Murch, she had precious little time to herself. She took her walk each day, though, something she had done, year in, year out, and couldn't miss whatever the weather, and in between whiles, she sat sewing, fashioning clothes for the two dolls. She was a good needlewoman and found pleasure in making the finicky little garments; she had the last one done on the day before Mr Trentham was to leave for London to collect his daughters. It had meant sitting up late to do it, but now the dolls were dressed and ready, and while the little girls were staying at the cottage she would find the time to knit another outfit for each of them. She saw him off after breakfast and it was only as an afterthought that he told her that he would be back about teatime.

The cottage seemed very empty once he had

roared away down the lane, but she reminded herself that she had a lot to do and would be free to do it when and where she chose. She went first and picked some late chrysanthemums, putting a great bowl of them in the sitting room and a smaller one in Miss Murch's bedroom, and that done, she began on scones and cakes for tea; a chocolate sandwich filled with whipped cream, another fruit cake because Mr Trentham liked those best and some little iced fairy cakes. By lunchtime she had the fires going, hot water bottles in the beds and the tea table laid with one of her grandmother's old-fashioned linen and crochet cloths. There wasn't a complete tea set any more, but the cups, saucers and plates, although all different, were old and delicate and pretty. Sadie felt satisfied with her efforts as she had her lunch, and then went upstairs to change out of her smock and put on her new skirt and one of the pretty blouses. Just for once she would have to forgo her walk, but she was too excited now to mind that.

It had been a dull day, now it was already dark, with a cold wind and the hint of rain. At four o'clock she switched on the lights and took up her position in the sitting room window where she had a sideways view of the lane. She didn't have to wait very long. She was at the door when she realised that it wasn't Mr Trentham's car at all, but a taxi, and the figure coming up the path certainly wasn't him. Sadie held the door wide and Miss Murch paused on the step. She was a tall woman, slim to the point of boniness, with a good deal of jet black hair showing beneath her little fur hat. She was faultlessly made up and her coat looked expensive; she looked like a model who was past it and who had no intention of giving up. Her pale blue eyes examined Sadie's small person with cool unfriendliness, so that Sadie was left in no doubt as to what the lady thought of her, all the same she said in her pleasant soft voice: 'Miss Murch? Do come in, you must be tired and cold. There's a fire in the sitting room.' She peered over one elegant shoulder. 'Are the children with you? I thought...'

'Naturally they are. They'll stay in the car until I send for them. Mr Trentham was delayed in town, he'll be following later. What's your name?'

'Sadie Gillard.' Sadie was determined to be friendly.

'Well, Gillard, you may fetch the children and tell the driver to bring in the luggage. I've paid him and I daresay he wishes to get back to Crewkerne as quickly as possible.'

Sadie, well brought up though she had been, almost bit her tongue to stop the retort which was ready on it. Only the thought of the children sitting out there in the cold dark kept her silent. She took her old coat from behind the kitchen door and went down the path, slippery with icy rain. The driver was sitting morosely behind the wheel and behind him, sitting close together, were two small girls. They looked cold and scared, and Sadie was instantly sorry for them. She nodded to the driver and opened the door. She said softly: 'Hullo, I'm Sadie, your father's housekeeper. Will you come into the house? There's a big fire and a lovely tea waiting.'

Neither of them answered, but they got out obediently and she gave them each a hand. 'Would you mind bringing in the luggage?' she asked the driver, 'and if you can stay a few minutes I'll give you your tea—you must be cold and it's quite a drive back.'

He was already getting out of the taxi. 'I reckoned her could fetch her own stuff, but I could do with a nice cuppa since you'm offered it so kindly.'

He went round the back of the taxi, and Sadie took the small hands wordlessly offered to her and went up the path and into the cottage.

Miss Murch had taken off her coat and was sitting in front of the fire. She looked strongly disapproving and said at once: 'Anna, Julie, take off your coats and hats and sit down quietly until tea is ready. Where are the cases?'

'They'll be here in a minute.' Sadie took the

coats and smiled at the children. 'Which one is Julie and which Anna?' she asked, and held out a hand.

Their small hands were cold and they looked cold too—not cold exactly, she corrected herself, just tired and in need of a good meal. Julie was dark with big brown eyes and straight hair and Anna was dark too, only her hair was curly and her eyes were hazel. They looked at Sadie suspiciously and then at Miss Murch. It was obvious to Sadie that they didn't like that lady and they were afraid of her too. She pulled the sofa nearer the fire and invited them to sit down, then went into the hall to find the driver surrounded by cases and bags. 'I'll take them up for you, Miss...'

'Oh, would you? You're very kind. Then come into the kitchen and have that tea.'

She gave him a mug full from the pot of tea she was making, piled a plate with scones and a slice of cake, and told him to sit down and eat it. 'I'll just go in with the tea, but I'll be back presently,' she assured him.

All three were sitting just as she had left them and in an effort to lighten the situation she said cheerfully: 'Tea is ready, will you come and sit down?'

Miss Murch cast a disparaging look at the table. 'I don't allow the children to eat rich cakes,' she stated.

'These aren't rich and they're home-made; just for once perhaps you'll relax your rules?' said Sadie, and passed the scones.

'You have your meals with us, Gillard?' asked Miss Murch. She had asked for tea with no milk or sugar and was nibbling a scone with every sign of loathing.

'I do, Miss Murch. I'm called Sadie, perhaps you will be kind enough to call me that.' She spread cream and jam lavishly on to scones and offered them to the little girls. 'Excuse me for a moment and I'll see if the driver has finished his tea.'

Miss Murch looked at her with horror. 'You've left him in the kitchen? He could ransack the place!'

'Don't be silly,' said Sadie, her nice manners swept away for the moment. 'This isn't wicked London, we don't steal from each other here.'

In the kitchen she found the man ready to go. 'And thank 'ee kindly, love,' he said, and jerked his head towards the sitting room door. 'I don't envy you—nasty old lady her be.'

'Did she give you a tip?' asked Sadie.

'Cor love 'ee, no!'

She went to the tea caddy on the shelf above the stove and took out a pound note. 'Well, here you are, and I'm sure you deserve it. Mind you go back carefully.'

'Bless you, love, and a merry Christmas.' He grinned at her and went off down the path whistling, 'Good King Wenceslas,' and Sadie went back to her tea.

Anna and Julie had empty plates and were eyeing the chocolate sponge. Sadie cut generous slices and offered them without saying a word to Miss Murch, but that lady was too occupied in looking around her to notice.

'I had no idea,' she began sharply, 'that this place would be so poky and primitive—if I had, I would have refused to bring the girls here.'

'Well, if their father wants them here for the holidays, you can't do much about it, I suppose?'

'I should have protested strongly. Mr Trentham has complete confidence in me, he would have taken my advice.'

It didn't sound like Mr Trentham, somehow.

'Is this the only sitting room?' asked Miss Murch. She looked at Sadie so accusingly that Sadie only just stopped herself apologising.

'That's right. Mr Trentham uses the dining room as his study and there's a kitchen.'

Miss Murch shuddered as though kitchens were a dirty word. 'I trust that I have a room to myself?' she asked with a little sneer.

'Yes, of course. If we've all finished our tea we

can go upstairs and you can unpack. Anna, Julie, will you help me take the things into the kitchen?'

The children cast sideways glances at Miss Murch, and since she had been taken by surprise and had nothing to say, they nodded and followed Sadie. Tom was in his usual chair and the two little girls crowded round him still silent but quite animated.

'You can both talk if you want to,' said Sadie matter-of-factly, 'Tom likes company and he's very gentle.'

'It's nice here,' said Anna after a moment, 'isn't it, Julie?' They both looked at Sadie. 'We like you. May we call you Sadie?'

'Well, of course you can. Let's go and get the rest of the things, shall we? We want a tidy room in case your father comes home soon.'

'He had to go to a lunch with someone, but he said he'd leave early.'

'Then he won't be long, will he?' Sadie led the way back into the sitting room and found Miss Murch sitting by the fire again. She had turned on the TV too.

'I'm quite exhausted,' she exclaimed. 'You might take the children with you into the kitchen; we can unpack when I've had a rest.'

'They're going to help me wash up—it takes a

long time with only one, you know. But I expect you'll help me with the supper things later.'

Miss Murch smoothed the sleeve of her cashmere sweater. 'I never wash up,' she observed.

'There's always a first time,' said Sadie with a pertness she was ashamed of, but somehow Miss Murch seemed to bring out the worst in her.

They went into the kitchen and shut the door, and miraculously the little girls became just like any other little girls. They giggled and listened enchanted to all the things Sadie had planned for Christmas. She was telling them about the candlelit service she would take them to down at the village church when the kitchen door opened very quietly and Mr Trentham came in. They didn't see him at once and when they did Sadie stopped in midsentence and the two children drew sharp breaths. They looked pleased to see him, but they looked nervous, and Sadie wondered why.

She said 'Good evening, Mr Trentham,' and watched while his small daughters advanced to kiss him. He looked ill at ease and so did they; surely they weren't shy of each other? He kissed them and looked at her over their heads. 'They've been such a help,' she told him, 'they wiped the plates so carefully, and Tom's delighted to have company.'

'Where's Miss Murch?'

'Isn't she in the sitting room? She was—she's

tired and thought she would rest before they un-pack.'

He looked as though he was going to speak, but instead he turned to go out of the room. Sadie stopped him at the door. 'Would you like some tea?' she asked. 'I know it's late, but I expect supper will be a bit later, won't it?' She glanced at the children. 'Do Anna and Julie stay up?'

Two small eager faces turned towards their father. 'Why not—just this once, since they've been so good.'

He left the door open and went into the sitting room and left that door open too. Sadie heard Miss Murch, presumably taken by surprise, exclaim in a sugary voice: 'Oh, Mr Trentham, how delightful that you're so early; there are several things I feel I simply must bother you with.'

Sadie shut the kitchen door; she felt sure that one of the things would be her. She thought with regret of the Miss Murch she had imagined and wondered how she would be able to bear the real Miss Murch's company until after Christmas. Not company, exactly, she corrected herself, Miss Murch obviously didn't consider her a social equal. She went to a drawer in the kitchen table and took out a pack of cards. 'Does anyone here play Snap?' she wanted to know, and was appalled to find that they didn't.

It took them about ten minutes to master the game. They were having the time of their lives when the door opened again and both Miss Murch and Mr Trentham came in.

'Oh, my dears!' cried Miss Murch. 'You shouldn't be sitting in this kitchen—come by the nice warm fire.'

Sadie hadn't been aware that she had a nasty side to her character; she had never had occasion to show it. Now it took over with a vengeance. She said gently: 'But, Miss Murch, you asked me to keep them here in the kitchen with me so that you could have a rest. We've been quite happy.'

Miss Murch's delicately tinted face became mottled. 'We'll go and unpack.' And the children got up and went obediently after her up the stairs. Mr Trentham hadn't said a word; now he closed the door very gently.

'I wonder if I have done the right thing, having the children down here.' He spoke with a deceptive blandness which she mistrusted.

'They'll love it once they're used to it. I daresay the cottage is different from your home in London.'

'Miss Murch seems to think so. She's appalled that there's no central heating.'

'Oh dear, but I put a hot water bottle in her bed, and the children's.'

'Not mine?' She thought he was laughing at her.

'It's too early for yours,' she told him. 'What time would you like supper, Mr Trentham?'

'As soon as possible. I lunched with a friend and everything seemed to be covered in sauce—I'm not sure what I ate.'

'Well, it's steak and kidney pudding for supper with Brussels sprouts and buttered parsnips and potatoes in their jackets, and I made a trifle for pudding—I thought the little girls might like that.'

'I'll like it too. Is there any sherry in it?'

'A tablespoonful.' She looked at him guiltily. 'I took it from the dining room—you weren't here to ask. I hope you don't mind.'

'I don't mind—I should have minded if you'd given me a trifle without sherry, though.' He looked round the kitchen. 'Are you sure you can manage, Sadie?'

She gave him a surprised look. 'Of course,' she smiled suddenly, 'especially if I'm going to have help with the washing up.'

Supper was a difficult meal. The food got eaten, of course, every last crumb, although Miss Murch refused the steak and kidney and had vegetables and biscuits and cheese instead of trifle, but the little girls gobbled up their portions with heartwarming gusto and Mr Trentham, as usual, enjoyed a good second helping. He had opened a bottle of claret too, but it hadn't done much to loosen their

tongues. Miss Murch carried on a genteel mono-
logue, name-dropping with every second breath and
constantly reminding Mr Trentham about this or
that distinguished person they had met. That he replied either not at all or with a grunt did nothing to
stop her; after a little while Sadie stopped listening
and planned the meals for the next day. The little
girls hardly spoke and then only in whispers; it puzzled Sadie that they looked at their father with such
adoring eyes and at the same time shied away from
him like frightened ponies.

Mr Trentham spooned the last of the trifle. 'It's
time you were in bed, my dears,' he said, cutting
ruthlessly into Miss Murch's account of how she
had coped with all the difficulties of the train journey that day. So they slid from their chairs and
kissed him rather shyly and then, almost without
hesitation, went and kissed Sadie too. She hugged
them with a lack of selfconsciousness, which made
Mr Trentham look thoughtfully at her. 'Goodnight,
darlings,' she said. 'Wouldn't it be fun if it snowed
tomorrow! We could make a snowman.'

Miss Murch was too ladylike to sniff, but she
registered disapproval. When she had gone, Sadie
said: 'I'm sorry, I shouldn't have said that about
snowmen—I didn't mean to encroach on Miss
Murch's ground.'

Mr Trentham leaned back in his chair and stared

at her. 'They like you,' he observed. 'Probably it's all those cakes for tea. I'm afraid Miss Murch doesn't approve of you, though.' His face was deadpan. 'They ate cake for tea and sat in the kitchen and played with Tom. I understand that cats are dirty animals.'

Sadie rose to the bait. 'What utter nonsense! Tom is cleaner than any of us—all cats are clean...' She stopped abruptly, biting her lip. 'I'm sorry, I'll keep out of their way as much as I can.'

'I think we might exempt Tom.' He got to his feet and started collecting plates.

'What are you doing?' asked Sadie, astonished.

'I suspect that my education has been neglected. I'm going to wash up!'

CHAPTER FOUR

IT WAS STILL quite dark when Sadie got up the next morning, but it had turned colder still during the night and the frost lay thick on the ground. She showered and dressed and crept downstairs, and made a cup of tea for herself before starting on the fires. She had become adept at doing this silently by now, just as she laid the table for breakfast with no sound at all before going into the kitchen to put on the porridge and put the frying pan on to heat up. By now there was a good deal of movement upstairs and presently Mr Trentham came down, poked his head round the kitchen door, demanded tea and went into the dining room; he was certainly a glutton for work. Sadie took in the tea and started on the bacon and was slicing bread when Anna and Julie came in. They wished her good morning in polite wooden little voices and then went to Tom, waiting for his breakfast.

'Would you like to put some milk in Tom's saucer?' asked Sadie. 'It's under the table there, so he can have his milk first and then a little bowl of porridge. Do you like porridge?'

They looked blank. 'It's nice,' she went on, 'we

81

have it every morning with lots of sugar and milk, and do you like bacon?'

They professed themselves willing to try anything and stood without making a sound while she ladled the porridge into bowls and carried the tray into the sitting room. 'Come and sit at the table,' she suggested. 'Your father will be here in a moment.'

She tapped on the door as she went past and he came out at once, kissed his children, enquired after their night and sat down to his breakfast. The porridge dealt with, Sadie fetched in bacon and eggs and the crisp fried bread that went well with it, and it was as he was serving this that he enquired where Miss Murch was.

'She said she couldn't get up until she'd had a cup of tea,' Anna gulped. 'She said Sadie was to take it up, only I forgot...'

Her father smiled at her. 'Never mind, poppet, it doesn't matter.' He got up from the table and went into the hall. 'Come down to breakfast, Miss Murch!' he bellowed. 'You'll need it—the children want to go for a walk and we've almost finished!'

Miss Murch appeared some twenty minutes later, elegant and well made up and in a cold fury. She wished Mr Trentham a chilly good morning, frowned at the children and ignored Sadie. 'Toast will do for me.' She sat down and poured herself a cup of coffee from Mr Trentham's pot.

'And when you've eaten it,' said Mr Trentham crisply, 'be good enough to come and see me in the dining room.'

He stalked out, and Sadie's heart sank; it wasn't going to be a success, this holiday. His routine which she had so carefully followed was being disorganised; worse, his very own coffee pot had been emptied by Miss Murch. She looked at the little girls and saw their forlorn faces. Living with Miss Murch couldn't be much fun for them, and she wondered if they were happy living with her in London. It was really too bad of Mr Trentham to ignore them: she wondered why. Perhaps he was so busy making a name for himself and lots of money that he had no time for them. But he already had a name for himself, and more than enough money... They were dear little girls too. She smiled at them and said: 'I saw a fox this morning, going up the hill behind the cottage.'

'What's a fox?' asked Julie, and when Sadie explained Miss Murch said crossly:

'It's all so primitive. Supposing I need to buy something, where do I go?'

'There's a shop in the village,' suggested Sadie, stubbornly friendly.

Miss Murch cast her a look of dislike. 'Not that kind of shop—I always go to Harrods.'

Unanswerable, thought Sadie, and left alone with the children after Miss Murch had crossed the hall on her high heels and tapped on the dining room door, suggested that they should all wash up. They were almost through, giggling and laughing and talking to Tom, when Miss Murch opened the door. 'You seem very anxious for the children to do the housework,' she said sourly. 'I must forbid them to come into the kitchen. You hear me, Anna, Julie? You are not to come in here with the housekeeper. Now come with me and we shall all go for a walk.'

The children looked imploringly at Sadie, but she said: 'You must do as Miss Murch asks, my dears, and you'll enjoy a walk.' She smiled brightly at them, Miss Murch included, but when they had gone the smile faded. It was going to be worse than she had imagined; Miss Murch was a petty tyrant, the children were milk and water shadows of what children should be and they didn't look happy. For the first time since she had met him, she allowed herself to be annoyed with Mr Trentham.

He came out for his coffee presently, coming into the kitchen and sitting at the table while she poured it out. 'Children gone out?' he wanted to know, and at her wordless nod: 'Why do you look like that?'

'Like what?'

'As cross as two sticks. Have you and Miss Murch been having words? She's a bit put out this morning: I daresay she finds it rather different from the house at Highgate. She'll settle down, I daresay.'

Sadie doubted that, but she wasn't going to say so, probably Miss Murch was a very good governess and he set great store by her. She stood at the sink peeling potatoes, saying nothing. It was Mr Trentham who did all the talking. His writing was going well, it seemed, he would have it finished in the next ten days. He was thinking of taking a short holiday before starting on a documentary for BBC 2. 'Somewhere warm,' he observed. 'Greece, or Corsica.' He added: 'I detest the weeks after Christmas.'

'We get snowdrops here in January,' said Sadie, and he laughed. 'Is that an inducement for me to stay here? What else?'

'Lambs—and the annual whist drive at the Vicarage, and the sales…'

'I don't think that I find any of those things very interesting.'

'No, I didn't think you would. I expect this cottage is fine for you when you're working, but in between you want to get back to your normal kind of life.'

He was watching her with a half smile. 'And what would that be, Sadie?'

'Oh, meeting interesting people—actresses and novelists and publishers—and going to the theatre and out to dinner in big restaurants and shopping at Harrods.'

'Harrods? I never go there. What should I buy there, in heaven's name? I've been going to Turnbull and Asser for years.'

Sadie had never heard of them. She said wistfully: 'There must be some gorgeous shops...'

'You've been in London, surely?'

'Oh, yes, Granny and I went with the WI about five years ago, but we didn't get further than Oxford Street.'

He said gently: 'Well, you must go again one day, but it's very noisy and crowded and you can't hear a bird sing, let alone a sparrow chirping.'

She said, almost defiantly: 'I'm happy here, but it would be nice just to see...I wouldn't want to live in London.'

'Do you know, I'm beginning to think that too.'

She waited for him to say more and was frustrated by the return of the walkers, none of whom were in a good humour. The little girls were cold, and their legs, encased in thin tights, were cold too. They were wearing all the wrong clothing—smart double-breasted cloth coats and velvet tammies:

just right for Highgate, probably, but not much use
in Chelcombe. And Miss Murch had fared even
worse, for she wore high-heeled suede boots, spat-
tered with icy mud, and her coat, although elegant,
just didn't suit her environment. She told the children sharply to take off their things and disappeared
upstairs to her room, where she stayed, only coming
down for coffee when Sadie had made hot cocoa
for the little girls and given them a biscuit each.
Their father, to Sadie's surprise, had stayed in the
kitchen, reading the paper and drinking more coffee, and exchanging a goodnatured, desultory conversation with his daughters. He was still there
when Miss Murch opened the door. 'Come out of
the kitchen at once!' she ordered the children, not
seeing Mr Trentham for the moment. 'And bring
me my coffee in the sitting room—and mind it's
hot!'

Mr Trentham looked up from his paper. 'The
children may stay here as long as they wish,' he
said gently, 'and there's plenty of hot coffee on the
stove. Help yourself, Miss Murch.'

Which she did, with an ill grace and a nasty look
at Sadie, who, busy making pastry for an apple pie,
didn't notice.

'Father Christmas is coming to Bridport in two
days' time,' she told the children, and cut off the

edges of pastry and divided them fairly into two. 'Here, make a pie each.'

'May we—real pies?'

'Why not? I'm sure your father will enjoy them.' She handed over a pot of mincemeat. 'There are two patty pans in that drawer, you can each make a mince pie.'

Julie had begun to roll her bit of pastry. 'Will Father Christmas come here? He goes to Harrods, I saw him last year.'

'Not here, in the village. He couldn't possibly visit every little village in the country.'

'So may we go to Bridport and see him?'

'Ask your Father,' suggested Sadie, and watched the newspaper being lowered to expose a cross face.

'I'm a busy man,' he objected, 'how can I possibly get my work done if I have to traipse after Father Christmas whenever I'm asked?'

'Just once,' wheedled Sadie. 'But of course—I'd forgotten your work. Luckily there's a bus going to Bridport just before noon, would you mind if I took Julie and Anna? We could come back on the afternoon bus and be back in time to get your tea. Perhaps Miss Murch would like to come too.'

'I doubt it.' His voice was dry. He gathered up the paper and got to his feet. 'If I'm left in peace for the rest of the day, then I'll drive you in—but mind, we're coming straight back the moment you've seen Father Christmas.'

The little girls rushed at him. 'Daddy, Daddy, will you really? When shall we go?'

'We'll be at the Town Hall at twelve o'clock sharp,' said Sadie. 'You'll have plenty of time to see him and be back for lunch—hot soup and pasties. I'll have it on the table waiting to be eaten.'

'No, you won't. You started on this, you're coming too.' Mr Trentham went through the door without another word or anyone having a chance to say anything.

It grew steadily colder during the day and the next day it snowed. Miss Murch roundly refused to take the children for a walk 'They'll catch their deaths of cold,' she observed, and made herself comfortable close to the sitting room fire as she could manage, leaving the children to amuse themselves. Naturally before long they were quarrelling and bored, and with the prospect of Mr Trentham's furious face appearing round the door at any moment, Sadie left her chores, put on her old coat and her wellies and got the children's coats and shoes. Probably they would be ruined and certainly wet, but anything was better than Mr Trentham's wrath. Without saying a word to Miss Murch, she stole out of the kitchen door, the two children creeping like mice behind her, and led them to the little patch of grass where she hung the washing, now nicely blanketed in snow.

They had never made a snowman. Breathless with excitement and the pleasure of being out of doors, they slavishly followed Sadie's instructions and before long had a rather lopsided figure more or less ready. Sadie was fashioning a nose when she dropped her handful of snow and spun round at Mr Trentham's voice.

'I distinctly heard Miss Murch say that the children weren't to go outside!' he snapped. He spoke pleasantly enough, but he looked like a thundercloud.

Sadie glanced guiltily at their snow-covered shoes and the telltale splashes where a snowball had found its mark on their coats, and then she looked at the two rosy faces. 'Yes, you did, Mr Trentham, but they got bored—they're children and they need to play; just imagine, they'd never had the chance to make a snowman before. I'm sorry if you're angry, but it's done them good.'

He stood looking at her, not saying a word, although she expected to be given her notice out of hand; she was only the housekeeper, easily replaced, whereas Miss Murch was probably a paragon among governesses.

He came through the door, still staring at her in an unnerving manner, and she braced herself and then let all her pent-up breath out as Miss Murch sailed majestically out of the kitchen. She was angry, so angry that she actually pushed Mr Trentham aside. 'How dare you!' she began. 'How dare you, a mere servant, deliberately disobey my orders? I'll have you dismissed...'

'A slight misunderstanding, Miss Murch,' said Mr Trentham softly. 'I gave permission for Julie and Anna to come out here with Sadie, and may I remind you that any dismissing that might be done will be done by me?'

He went back into the house and Miss Murch, giving Sadie a dagger glance, went after him. Sadie swallowed. She was going to be sacked when it was convenient to Mr Trentham to do so, in the meantime she would have to behave as usual. She said cheerfully: 'Let's finish his face, my dears, and then we'll find an old hat and a scarf—I'm sure there's something in the shed that will do.'

So they finished their snowman, and the little girls, after a few minutes' uneasiness, forgot all about the few moments' unpleasantness and presently went back into the house, where Sadie took off their coats and shoes, and did the best she could to restore them to their pristine state. But even though she restored them she couldn't restore Miss Murch's temper. That lady refused to speak to her and during lunch carried on an animated conver-

sation with Mr Trentham and afterwards swept the
two little girls into the sitting room for a reading
lesson. As for Mr Trentham, he didn't speak to Sadie at all, except to tell her that he would be out
for dinner that evening. She was laying the table
for their supper when he came into the room, elegant in his black tie and more aloof in his manner
than he had ever been. There was no doubt about
it that he was going to give her the sack. She waited
for the fatal words and was very taken aback when
he asked her to sew a button on his jacket. It wasn't
off, only loose, but she tightened it neatly without
saying a word, and when he thanked her and wished
her goodnight, she said goodnight in a calm voice,
although her insides were shaking. He would wait
until the morning, she supposed.

She supposed wrong. Beyond greeting her at the
breakfast table, he had nothing to say and the meal
was eaten in a silence punctuated by Miss Murch's
frequent admonishments to the children. She had
been worse than awful the previous evening. Sadie,
a mild girl by nature, had longed to throw something at her, but mindful of the children, she had
held her tongue and listened to her companion talking at her for the length of the meal. It was a great
relief when the meal had been eaten and she had
been able to retire to the kitchen and wash up and
presently go to bed, leaving Miss Murch sitting cos-

ily by the fire, a book in her hand and a glass of
Mr Trentham's port beside her.

But whatever had been decided about her own
future, the trip to Bridport was still on. When she
took in the coffee she was reminded to be ready to
leave the house, and with Mr Trentham standing,
as it were, with a stopwatch in his hand and making
sure that everyone was on time, they all got into
the car and were driven off rather faster than Sadie
considered safe along the narrow country lanes, although she would never have dared to say so.

It was impossible not to be infected by the festive
air which enveloped Bridport. Even Miss Murch's
muttered asides about yokels and their childish
pleasures couldn't spoil their fun. Sadie wormed her
way well to the front of the people lining the main
street and stood with a small hand in each of hers
and cheered as loudly as the children round her
when Father Christmas, standing in the back of an
open car, drove slowly past.

Miss Murch looked the other way. Harrod's Father Christmas was to be tolerated since he was
patronised by the upper crust, but this country ver-
sion, even if his white whiskers were his own,
didn't merit a glance. And as for Mr Trentham, he
hardly noticed him; his eyes were resting thoughtfully upon Sadie's face. It could of course be the
new coat and the beret, but it seemed to him that

she was quite a pretty girl, not to be compared with the elegant lovely young women he knew in London—but then none of them, as far as he knew, could cook so much as an egg.

The procession was quickly over and people started making their way back home or to finish the shopping. Miss Murch took the little girls' hands and began to walk them impatiently to the car park down the street, but Mr Trentham said: 'Not so fast, Miss Murch! I think we could all do with a hot drink,' and led the way into the Greyhound Hotel behind them where they sat in its cosy, old-fashioned coffee room and the children chattered happily, so that the lack of conversation between the grown-ups hardly mattered. They included Sadie in their giggling talk, though, asking her any number of questions which she answered promptly, if not always quite truthfully, but Miss Murch would have nothing to do with such nonsense and presently began her own conversation with Mr Trentham, who answered her politely but mostly in words of one syllable which made it difficult to continue. On the whole, it was a relief when they had finished their coffee and cocoa and were ready to go home. There was a delay while the children begged to look at the shops, an idea quickly and far too sharply rejected by Miss Murch, and since Mr Trentham pointed out that he had a luncheon engagement at old Lady Benson's house just outside the village, there was nothing for it but to get into the car. Sadie had toyed with the idea of asking if she and the children could stay in Bridport for lunch and an hour's shopgazing and return on the afternoon bus, but Mr Trentham's face looked so severe that she decided against it.

Lunch was an uncomfortable meal. Miss Murch was plainly in a very bad temper and determined to take it out on everyone near her. She found fault with the little girls and went on and on about the discomforts of living in an isolated village where there was no restaurant, no cinema even, and as far as she could ascertain, no theatre within miles. And as for shops…she raised her eyes to the ceiling. 'I shall be glad when Christmas is over and we're safely back at Highgate,' she observed. 'I miss my friends.'

Sadie, determined to keep friendly at all costs, asked: 'Do the children have lots of friends? I expect they do…' She smiled at the children and wished they would smile back. They were such dears but so ungetatable.

'I am careful to choose suitable children for Julie and Anna to play with,' said Miss Murch repressively. 'I've seen no children around here.'

'Dozens of them in the village,' pointed out Sadie. 'They'll be on holiday in a day or two, there are sure to be one or two the children will like.'

'I decide with whom they shall play,' declared Miss Murch, 'and now, if you will clear this table, Julie and Anna can get out their drawing books. There's no need to go for a walk this afternoon, thank heavens.'

There was no sign of Mr Trentham, Sadie got the tea at the usual time and had cleared it away before he walked in, only to tell her that he had met the Durrants at Lady Benson's and would be dining with them.

Sadie's heart sank. The prospect of a long evening with Miss Murch for company appalled her. Later, she watched Mr Trentham leave the house once more and wished heartily that she could have crept into his coat pocket.

And it was every bit as bad as she had expected. The children were almost silent throughout supper and her own attempts to get someone to talk failed lamentably, and after the little girls had been taken up to bed she spent as long as possible in the kitchen, and after half an hour sharing the sitting room with a silent Miss Murch, she went to bed herself.

She didn't go to sleep, though; it was much later when she heard the car and Mr Trentham's firm steps up the garden path. He must have joined Miss

Murch in the sitting room, for she could hear their voices, they were still talking when she finally fell asleep.

She wasn't sure what woke her some hours later. She lay in bed trying to remember what kind of a sound it had been; that there was something she was sure, for Tom was sitting on the end of her bed with his ears on the alert. She got out of bed and put on her dressing gown and slippers and leaving the bedside light on, opened the door and crept downstairs.

It was a bright moonlight night and very cold so that the rooms downstairs were light enough. There was no one in the sitting room and the dining room door was shut, but the kitchen door was just a little open and she opened it wider. Julie was sitting in the old chair by the stove and Sadie slipped quickly inside and shut the door. 'It's all right, darling, it's only me. Don't you feel well?' She had whispered to the child, anxious not to frighten her and still more anxious not to rouse Miss Murch. And when there was no answer: 'I'm going to put on the light.'

Julie was crying, her face was blotched and wet and although the kitchen was still warm from the day's cooking, she was wearing only a nightie and no slippers. Sadie picked her up and sat her on her lap. 'Tell me all about it,' she invited comfortably, and began to rub the icy little feet.

'Daddy didn't say goodnight.'

'Well, love, he wasn't here…'

'He's never here. Miss Murch told him that she tucks us up at bedtime, but she never does—he think's she's as good as a mummy.' A fresh stream of tears rushed. 'She's horrid! I hate her, so does Anna. I wish you were our mummy, Sadie, and we could live here with you and Daddy for ever and ever.'

'But your daddy is a busy man, love, he has to work so that you can have clothes and nice things to eat.'

'Miss Murch says we can't live with him because we make too much noise. Sadie, will you ask him if we can stay here? We'll be ever so good.' Julie buried her face against Sadie's shabby red dressing gown, so it was only Sadie who saw the door open and Miss Murch standing there.

'I heard you!' she hissed. 'Turning the children against me, worming your way in! What are you after, I wonder? Getting them to like you and then setting your sights on their father, I shouldn't wonder! You're nothing but a fool—and a plain one too. Just you wait until the morning, my girl! Mr Trentham isn't going to like it when I tell him how you got the child out of bed and brought her down here in the cold and made her cry!'

'But that's not true!' cried Sadie. She was holding Julie tightly and the child had flung her arms round her neck.

'Oh, it'll sound true enough, and he listens to me.' Miss Murch smiled with a curled lip. 'I'll tell him why you did it too—in the hope that he would hear you and come downstairs and find you looking so touchingly maternal.' She tittered. 'I'll tell him that you confided in me, and I'll be so sympathetic and point out that it would be kinder to give you the sack than to let you stay on here, mooning after him.'

'Very ingenious, Miss Murch—what a pity I overheard you.' Mr Trentham, still in the beautifully tailored grey suit he had worn that evening, was standing in the hall. 'Be good enough to go to bed at once; I don't want Anna disturbed. I'll see you in the morning. Julie, I'm going to carry you up to bed, and we must be like mice so that we don't wake Anna.' His eyes studied Sadie in her dowdy dressing gown, her hair a fine curtain round her shoulders, her eyes huge in her pale face. 'Go to bed, Sadie,' he said, suddenly brisk.

Bed was cold, and Sadie picked up Tom and hugged him close. Mr Trentham had been angry, she knew the signs by now; he would give Miss Murch a good telling off in the morning and she herself would be told to go. He would be nice about it because he was fair enough to know that it hadn't been her fault, but it was an undisputable fact that she and Miss Murch didn't like each other, and the children had to be considered first. He might let her stay until after Christmas, but she doubted it. She wasn't indispensable—after all, they had spent other Christmases in hotels and they could again. Such a waste, she thought unhappily; all those puddings she had been going to make, and the lovely crackers and carefully thought out menus. She wiped away tears with an angry hand; only little girls cried. She went to sleep finally and woke with a headache.

She crept downstairs at her usual time in the morning and set about her chores. Breakfast was almost ready and she was laying the table when Miss Murch came down. She was elegantly dressed as she always was and carefully made up, and she was smiling, although her eyes were as hard as stones.

She wished Sadie good morning and without waiting for an answer went on in a hushed voice: 'I do apologise for the fuss I made last night. The truth is, I sleep so badly and waking suddenly and coming down here and finding Julie—the children are my first concern, you know. I'm sure we can come to some arrangement,' she went on. 'You can't possibly be happy here. I know of several good families who would love a housekeeper—in

London too. Think of the money you would earn and the clothes you could buy, and sooner or later you would meet some nice man and get married.' She shrugged her shoulders. 'You don't have to marry nowadays, of course, as long as you're reasonably discreet.' She came nearer to Sadie, who edged away. 'Now, surely we can come to an agreement. Suppose you give in your notice? You can tell Mr Trentham you want to spread your wings a bit, see the bright lights... He'll let you go, one housekeeper is very like another, you know. I'll give you enough money to keep you going for a few weeks...'

'You're bribing me?' said Sadie.

'Oh, no, my dear, just offered to help.'

Mr Trentham, who had come downstairs early to do some work and had been in the hall listening to this conversation, thought it time to intervene. 'I seem fated to overhear the most extraordinary conversations,' he observed irritably. 'Miss Murch, I must admire your ingenious plans, but I'm afraid they won't do. I've given the matter some thought and I've decided to send the girls to school here. They seem to me to be singularly lacking in the usual childish pleasures, perhaps a few friends of their own age will remedy that. This being so, I'm sure you'll be only too glad to return to London at once so that you can spend a civilised Christmas.

Have your breakfast and come and see me, will you? I'll give you a cheque and drive you to Crewkerne when you're ready.'

Miss Murch had the glazed look of someone who had been hit on the head. 'You can't mean that, Mr Trentham!'

'Indeed I do, Miss Murch. Sadie, bring me a cup of coffee in the dining room and go and help the children finish dressing. I'll have breakfast with them later on.'

He went into the dining room and closed the door, and Sadie, quite speechless, carried in his coffee. He didn't look up when she went in, nor did he speak. She went upstairs and brushed the little girls' hair and helped them with zips and shoelaces, and when they went down presently, Miss Murch wasn't there. From the thumpings and banging going on in her room she was packing.

Breakfast wasn't nearly as bad as she had expected. Mr Trentham talked to his little daughters although he had very little to say to her, only when they had finished he said: 'Leave these things, Sadie, and take the children down to the village, or for a walk, and don't come back for a couple of hours.'

He didn't smile at her, but she was relieved to see that he grinned at the children and bent to kiss them as he got up from the table.

It irked her very much to leave the dirty dishes, but she got the children into their hats and coats, fetched her own coat and a headscarf and started off for the village. It was lucky that there was a small amount of shopping to be done; they could spend a little time with Mrs Beamish.

The village shop might be small, but Mrs Beamish had stocked it well for Christmas. Sadie made her few purchases and then gave the children fifty pence each to spend. They had looked so surprised that she had explained: 'It's pocket money, my dears—I expect you get it every week, don't you?'

They shook their heads, and Anna asked: 'May we buy things, Sadie?'

'Of course you may. Choose what you want as long as it doesn't cost more than you've got.'

Which took quite a time, but presently, their cheeks bulging with toffee, they said goodbye to Mrs Beamish and followed Sadie down the steps and into the village street. 'Which way?' they asked.

'Let's go through the village and look at the duckpond and then we'll peep into the church; they'll be putting up the Christmas tree soon. If your father will allow it, I'll take you to the carol service.'

She had thought at first that two hours was going to be a long time to fill in, but she need not have

worried. They walked all round the pond, spent
quite a time in the church and then called on Mrs
Coffin to get another dozen eggs, and since Mrs
Coffin didn't have many visitors they stayed drinking cocoa in her stuffy sitting room while the children admired the dozens of china ornaments and
then helped put the eggs carefully in Sadie's basket.
It was well past the two hours Mr Trentham had
decreed by the time they got back to the cottage.

The door wasn't locked and they went in cautiously. Perhaps Miss Murch hadn't gone after all,
thought Sadie; Mr Trentham might have had second
thoughts. He hadn't; he came out of the dining
room as they stood in the hall. He said cheerfully,
'There you are. Get your things off and come into
the sitting room, we're going to hold a serious discussion.'

CHAPTER FIVE

SOMEONE HAD cleared the breakfast things off the table. The children scampered to their chairs and sat looking expectantly at their father as Sadie took a seat opposite him. She had no idea what he was going to say, but she had braced herself against the news. Mr Trentham liked utter quiet while he was working, an impossibility without a governess to look after his small daughters, which meant that they would go back to Highgate or, what was more likely, there would be another governess or even an au pair coming. Well, anyone would be better than Miss Murch.

'May I have your undivided attention?' asked Mr Trentham with impatient civility, so that she went a guilty pink and stammered: 'Yes, yes, of course, Mr Trentham—so sorry...'

He didn't smile at her, but he did at the children, which she took as a good sign, nor did he sit down, but began to pace up and down the room, flinging words at them from over his shoulder.

'Miss Murch has returned to London. She will not be coming back; she found the country did not agree with her. I propose to send you, Anna, and you, Julie, to the village school for a year or so, and you will live here permanently, although it seems reasonable to suppose that we'll spend the school holidays in Highgate. When you've out-grown the school here we'll review the situation. But all this depends on Sadie.' He paused in front of her and bent a frowning gaze upon her startled face.

'Do I ask too much of you, I wonder? To run the cottage and look after Anna and Julie as well? Re-member I shall still demand utter quiet while I'm working and you'll have little leisure. I shall, of course, pay you more and we must come to some arrangement whereby you have a certain amount of free time each week, and some sort of stand-in must be arranged so that you can get any help you need.'

Sadie could hardly wait for him to finish. 'Oh, I'd like that very much,' she assured him, 'that is if you think I'll do and the children want me to stay.'

He gave her a rare, kind smile. 'We all want you to stay, Sadie.'

She looked at the little girls and was reassured by their pleased faces. She would be taking on quite a job, but at least it was a worthwhile one and in her own home. 'Then thank you,' she told him, 'I'll stay.'

Mr Trentham went and sat down at the table,

facing her. 'Splendid. Now there are several things to discuss. I've already made enquiries about the school. The new term starts in the middle of January, which gives us all time to shake down and see to one or two things. Sadie, I don't think the children have the right clothes...'

'No, they haven't. Kilts and woollies and tights or trousers, anoraks and Wellington boots and lace-up shoes, warm nighties, woolly gloves...'

'You'll see to that. We'll go shopping tomorrow. Where?'

'Dorchester or Yeovil, there's a Marks and Spencer there.' She broke off to listen to Julie who wanted red boots and Anna who wanted everything green.

'You shall both choose,' she promised.

Two pairs of eyes were turned on their father. 'You'll come too, Daddy?'

'Well, I suppose I'd better, then I can pay the bills, can't I?' He turned to Sadie. 'There are several things needed. A new washing machine, a new Hoover, electric fires for the bedrooms, the shed in the garden leaks and we need another lock on the back door. The whole place wants painting, and we must have a new thatch.'

'No, not now, you can't,' observed Sadie. 'You'll need dry weather for that. But old Martin and his son in the village would do the painting as soon as the weather's right. The thatcher you'll have to book,' she added. 'It costs an awful lot of money.'

The way he said, 'Thank you for your good advice,' sent the blood into her cheeks. He had a horrid way of making her feel foolish; she wouldn't utter another word.

Mr Trentham watched the blush fade before he spoke. 'There's one other thing, Sadie. Would Tom mind if we were to have a dog?'

Joyful shrieks from the children prevented her from saying anything for a moment. 'I shouldn't think so. Would it be a puppy or a grown-up dog?'

'I thought we might go to the nearest dogs' home and see when we get there. We've never had a dog in Highgate, at least not since my marriage, and after my wife died there was no one to take a dog for walks—I was seldom home, and Miss Murch disliked them. Of course, Anna and Julie must look after him. You'll have enough to do, Sadie.'

She looked at the two excited little faces. 'I'm sure Tom can be persuaded, especially if we take care to spoil him for a bit,' and they beamed at her. The difference in the little girls was really remarkable; it was amazing what Miss Murch's absence was doing for them.

Mr Trentham broke in on her thoughts. 'Lunch?' he queried. 'I should like to get in a few hours' work...' For all the world as though they had been preventing him.

She got up from the table. 'Soup and toasted cheese,' she said, 'if you two will lay the table.'

The children had a lot to say during lunch—Christmas, the dog, their new clothes; there was no end to their chatter, and Mr Trentham laid himself out to be charming. He was tolerant of their piping voices, made jokes, discussed the presents they should buy and generally behaved as a father should. Sadie was a little astonished, but holding to the theory that one should not push one's luck, she whisked the children into the kitchen to help with the dishes and then took them off to the village. Mrs Beamish had a nice old-fashioned assortment of paper chains, the sort one had to make oneself and gum together. They spent a long time choosing them and when they got back to the cottage they crept in and sat like mice in the sitting room, absorbed in their handiwork, speaking in whispers and giggling softly. They were still happily engaged when the typewriter stopped abruptly and Mr Trentham flung open the door and shouted: 'Where's the tea, then?'

When Sadie came back with the tray from the kitchen she found him sitting with the children, making a paper chain for himself.

'I had no idea these things still existed—I used

to make them when I was a small boy, my sister Cecilia was forever telling me how badly I did them, too.'

Sadie considered that he was making rather a botch of it now, but nothing on earth would have made her say so; just to see him sitting there making paper chains was nice.

'Where's Aunt Cecilia?' asked Julie.

'At her villa in Cannes, my dear, conserving her strength for the excitements of Christmas at Kingsley Park.' He dismissed the lady with a wave of the hand, and asked, 'Crumpets for tea?'

'Yes, Mr Trentham. We'll have to have tea round this small table, if you don't mind, the chains might get muddled up if we try to move them.'

Tea was a boisterous meal with the children getting a little too excited and Mr Trentham not seeming to mind. It was Sadie who suggested that since they were all going shopping in the morning, the little girls should have their baths and get ready for bed before supper so that they could go to bed immediately after.

'A splendid idea,' observed their father. He got up and went to the dining room. At the door he said: 'I'll be out for dinner, Sadie. You two can creep in and say goodnight before you go to bed.'

Later, listening to the car roaring off much too fast down the lane, Sadie wondered where he was going. He had many friends by now, of course, and a good-looking man, famous in his own field and unencumbered by a wife, would be much in demand. She sighed as she put her solitary supper on a tray and carried it through to the sitting room. She had her daydreams like any other normal girl, but they had never worried her overmuch, but now she found herself wishing fervently that they might come true just once. Dining and dancing with a handsome man and herself in a beautiful dress, turned into a beauty overnight, queening it over everyone within sight. 'Don't be ridiculous!' Sadie told herself loudly, and started to clear away the paper chains. They were in a hopeless tangle and Mr Trentham's was only half finished. She unravelled them patiently and laid them in a large box ready to finish the next day.

Of course, very little got done the next day. Its short daylight hours were taken up with getting to Dorchester, shopping from the long list Sadie had made, eating their lunch and allowing the little girls to buy Christmas presents. Sadie found it sad that there were so few people they wanted to give presents to, but they spent a long time buying socks and a simply shocking tie for their father, and Sadie obligingly admired a very gaily patterned headscarf, which she felt sure she would be wearing after Christmas Day.

The vexed question of a present for Miss Murch was debated and settled out of hand by Mr Trentham, who decreed that a card was sufficient. 'And don't forget your Aunt Cecilia,' he reminded them. So they spent another twenty minutes or so making up their minds at the handkerchief counter and after that a further ten minutes while they took Sadie apart in turn and asked her advice as to what they should give each other. She'd already thought of that; and with an eye to Mr Trentham's desire for quiet, suggested modelling clay and a painting book and paintbox. Their father whisked them away then, looking mysterious, and she was left free to nip back to Longmans' bookshop and buy something she had seen there during the morning—a large book which with care and patience could be turned into an Edwardian town house, complete with family, servants and furniture; guaranteed to keep everyone absorbed for hours on end, she hoped.

She wondered what Mr Trentham had bought the children; probably they had all the toys they wanted in London. Sooner or later he would have to go there and bring some of them back, she supposed, for there was no question of the house at Highgate being given up—indeed, she had already faced the prospect of him wishing to go back there once his scripts were finished; he would want to go out and about and see his friends again, travel perhaps. He would sell the cottage and the little girls would be sent to a boarding school and he would be free to lead a bachelor's life until he started to write something else. And she—she had no doubt at all that when the time came, if it suited him, he would give her a splendid reference, a month's wages and forget her.

It was fortunate that she had no more time for these gloomy thoughts, for when she got to the Judge Jeffreys restaurant where she was to meet them for tea, they were already there, the children very giggly and excited, their father still, she was thankful to see, tolerantly goodnatured.

She had left a casserole in the oven and a rice pudding, creamy and stuffed with raisins, with it, so that once they were back home there was little to do save lay the table, while the children undid all the parcels and then went upstairs with their own purchases and strict instructions to Sadie not to look.

Mr Trentham had gone straight into the dining room and shut the door, and she heard the clink of glass as he poured himself a drink. Sadie, whose drinking had been limited to birthdays and Christmas and the occasional party, wouldn't have minded one herself. She was tired and after supper there would be the children to put to bed, the dishes to wash and all the new clothes to be put away, and it would all have to be done without a sound, because he was at the typewriter again.

She gave the potatoes a vicious prod as the door was opened by a shrewd kick from Mr Trentham's large foot as she became aware that the typing had ceased.

He had a bottle in one hand and a couple of glasses which he put carefully on the table. 'I had no idea that little girls in large doses could be so tiring. A glass of sherry is the least I can offer you, you must be worn to a thread.'

He filled the glasses and handed her one and toasted her silently. She took a good sip and then another one, savouring the fragrant dryness, 'Oh, how very nice,' she said inadequately, and he smiled, so that she went on, not wishing to appear ungrateful: 'I don't know anything about sherry, or anything else for that matter.'

He smiled again. 'No, I know. Don't drink it too fast, it's quite heady.'

She had already discovered that. There was a pleasant wave of lighthearted warmth washing over her; the sips she had taken had been large ones, there wasn't much left in the glass and she should have refused when he filled it again. 'Don't worry, I won't let you get tipsy,' he assured her. 'Did you enjoy your day?'

'Very much, and so did the little girls, didn't

they? Thank you for sparing the time to take us, Mr Trentham.'

'Did you buy anything for yourself, Sadie?'

She gave him a surprised look. 'Me? Why, no, but I will later on. The sales will be at the end of December and I'll buy some more clothes then.'

'I'll drive you in to Dorchester again if you like, you can get what you want straight away.'

She shook her head and took a cautious sip of sherry. 'Thank you, but there's no need. I've got a new dress for Christmas and a blouse I've not even worn yet.'

He was watching her gravely, but she had the uneasy feeling that he was laughing at her behind the gravity. 'We might get asked out to a party.'

'Well, I shan't, though I expect you'll get any number of invitations. Lady Benson and Mrs Durrant call sometimes, or they did when Granny was alive, but we don't get asked to their houses. Sometimes I've been to Mr Frobisher's house for lunch and several times to a social evening…'

'What on earth's that?'

'Well, everyone in the village goes, and we all sit and talk and sometimes someone gives us a lecture and we have sandwiches and coffee…'

Mr Trentham's lips twitched. 'Have you ever been out to dinner with a man, Sadie?'

She considered, her memory slightly clouded by

sherry. 'Well, no, not just on my own—I used to go to the Young Farmers' annual dinner and dance, but when Granny couldn't get around any more, I stopped going.'

'And the theatre?'

'Oh, yes—I went with the WI to the Weymouth Operatic Society's production of *The Gondoliers*—it was very good. And I've been to Lyme Regis several times, there's a small theatre there—but not much else.'

Mr Trentham got up abruptly from where he had been sitting on the kitchen table. 'I'm going to London tomorrow, I shall probably not be back for a couple of days. Will you be able to manage?'

'Yes, of course.' Sadie wondered what he would say if she said no, she couldn't.

She told herself during the next couple of days that it was a good thing he wasn't in the house, because the children were able to get over their first excitement over their new clothes and run up and down stairs as much as they liked with the presents they had bought, now being packaged in gaudy paper and crooked Sellotape and laboriously labelled. And it gave her the chance to see to the puddings, make the cake and get old Martin up from the village to see to the leak in the shed; Mr Trentham would never have borne with the hammering.

All the same it was terribly quiet without Mr

Trentham roaring for his meals when he wasn't thumping his typewriter. She cleaned out the dining room, too, taking care to replace everything just where she had found it, even the piles of books and papers on the floor, and when she had finished, she sidled up the table and took a look at the sheet of paper in the typewriter. There were a few words only: *A Girl to Love*, he had written, and although she looked for the sheet that must have preceded it, she couldn't find it anywhere. Feeling guilty, she picked up her dusters and polish and went back to the kitchen, feeling as though Mr Trentham's grey eyes were on her back.

The two days became three. The little girls had finished their parcelling up and Sadie, to keep them occupied, had given them dough and told them to make mince pies. But even that had palled after a time, so they had put on their anoraks and wellington boots and Sadie had got into her old coat and they had gone for a long walk. Up the hill to the top and a look at the view and then down again, with the prospect of buttered toast for tea. It had got cold, cold enough to have snow, Sadie had said and she doubted very much if Mr Trentham would be home before the next day: 'So you shall have your supper,' she promised, 'and while I'm getting it, you can finish those paper chains.'

The walk had given them an appetite: 'Sausages

and chips,' said Julie, and, 'Bacon and eggs,' chipped in Anna, 'with fried bread.'

So when tea was done and they had sat for a while and watched *Blue Peter* and Sadie had shown them how to make the paper chains more elaborate, she went into the kitchen and got out the frying pan. The sausages were done to a turn and so was the bacon, and she had just started on the chips when she heard the car. The children heard it too. They flew to the door and flung it wide, letting in a stream of icy air, shrieking a welcome to their father. She heard him laughing and the door bang, and then he was in the kitchen, his dark head powdered with the snow that she had forecast.

'What a welcome!' he declared, and smiled down at Anna and Julie, hanging on to his jacket. 'You've never done that before.'

It was Anna who replied. 'Miss Murch wouldn't let us, she said that you were never to be disturbed and that you didn't like to be kissed or hugged.'

'Did she indeed?' He looked at Sadie, a pinny tucked round her small person, carefully turning her chips. 'And what do you say to that, Sadie?'

'I shouldn't think there was anything nicer than being kissed by your own children,' she said calmly.

He took off his jacket. 'Drag that into the sitting room and look in the pockets, there's something for

each of you,' and as the children rushed out: 'There
are several things just as nice,' he said softly. He
took the fork from her hand and laid it on the table
and put his arms round her. 'This, for instance,' and
he kissed her.

Sadie stood quite passive, in his arms, looking
up at him with her lovely eyes. She said in a clear
little voice: 'People do strange things at Christmas—the—the festive spirit and all that...'

He was smiling at her with the faintly mocking
kindness she found so disturbing. 'Wise Sadie, let
us by all means call it the festive spirit.' He let her
go with a casual movement. 'Whatever it is you're
having for supper smells good. Will there be
enough for me?'

'Of course. I've still got the eggs to do, the children chose what they wanted.' It was a relief to talk
about normal things. Being kissed like that had
shaken her badly—only, she told herself; because
no one had kissed her in such a fashion before;
the kisses at the Young Farmers' dance, and they
weren't all that in number, hadn't been like that at
all.

He sauntered away presently, leaving her to cook
more of everything while the children laid the table,
and over supper he entertained them with an account of the Christmas lights in Regent Street and

how lovely the shops were. But not a word as to what he had been doing or who he had been with.

Whatever it was, it must have inspired him to work harder than ever. He was downstairs before breakfast, demanding tea before banging the door on himself and his typewriter. But he came out when the bacon was sizzling in the pan and made himself amiable over breakfast, teasing the children, discussing the chances of the snow lasting, making a few commonplace remarks to Sadie about more logs, the telephone which was to be installed that very morning and the need to put some ashes outside the back door to cover the icy patches there. Looking at him stealthily, she found it hard to imagine him as he had been on the previous evening, holding her close and kissing her. He'd been glad to be home, she told herself sensibly, and resolutely shut out the picture of lovely ladies in London.

The snow started again after breakfast, and Sadie, tearing mouselike round the cottage tidying up while the little girls had another go at the paper chains, decided that a walk before lunch would be a good idea. She made the coffee, left it to keep warm on top of the stove, put a note on the kitchen table asking Mr Trentham to help himself and crept upstairs for the children's anoraks and gloves. They were leaving the cottage in the stealthiest of manners when Mr Trentham opened his door.

'Where are you all going?' he roared.

'For a walk.' Sadie didn't allow the roar to upset her; it was, after all, only a loud voice.

'I'm going with you.' He was already getting into his sheepskin jacket. 'I need inspiration as well as exercise.' He looked at Sadie, 'that's if you'll have me?'

'Well, of course we will. We thought we'd go to the top of the land and out across the field and go and see if Mrs Coffin has got any eggs.'

It was hardly a walk. They ran, and threw snowballs, and the children fell about laughing, behaving like normal children now. By the time they got to the top of the hill they had rosy cheeks and so had Sadie, and once in the field, they stopped to make a snowman, all four of them, making quite a good job of it. They were breathless as they reached Mrs Coffin's gate and it was Mr Trentham who suggested that only Sadie should go in. 'We're rather a crowd,' he pointed out.

'She'll be hurt if you don't,' Sadie pointed out. 'You're a celebrity in the village, and she'll be able to boast to all her friends that you've been to see her.'

She was right, of course. Mrs Coffin welcomed them with delight and they all trooped into her small sitting room, leaving their boots in the porch, then sat in her old-fashioned plush-covered chairs and drank the cocoa she insisted on making for them. Presently the children were allowed to go up the garden to collect the eggs from the nesting boxes while Mr Trentham entertained his hostess with London gossip. He did it very nicely and Sadie's heart warmed towards him; he was thoughtless and arbitrary and liked everything done the moment he said so, but he could be kind too.

Mrs Coffin's old eyes sparkled. As they said goodbye she said happily: 'I dunno when I've had such a day, not since the Queen Mum's birthday and Mr Frobisher lent me his black and white telly.'

Which was funny but a bit pathetic too.

Christmas came rushing at them from snowy skies—the candlelit carol service; the children's party at the Primary Church School to which Anna and Julie went, shy at first, and then joining in the games like all the other children. The carol singers, plodding up to the front door and being asked in to drink coffee and eat mince pies, the last-minute tying up of parcels and, for the first time in years, a great many Christmas cards. Mr Trentham had, it seemed, an inexhaustible number of friends and acquaintances.

And of course there were local dinner parties to which he went. Sadie was constantly washing and ironing dress shirts and offering black coffee in the morning as Mr Trentham's temper frayed at its edges.

'It's as bad as town,' he grumbled at her, on his way out for the third time in a row, 'and some of the food is atrocious.'

But Sadie was pleased when he refused several invitations for Christmas Eve. The children were in such a state of excitement that she was hard put to it to keep them occupied, and it was with a sigh of relief that she saw the three of them starting off for a walk after their lunch. It gave her a chance to make her last-minute preparations for the next day and set out the small table in the sitting room with little dishes of sweets and nuts and fruit. The chains they had hung with Mr Trentham's help a day or two earlier, and what with holly festooning the walls and Christmas candles on the mantelpiece and the tree in pride of place between the two windows, the room was more than comfortably full. The children had wanted to put the cards on every available surface too, but Sadie had persuaded them against that and instead had suggested that they should be pinned on to red paper streamers hanging down the walls of the hall. It had taken quite a time to hang them all up and she had got a little tired of the messages inside them. It seemed that Mr Trentham knew a great many girls who regarded him with the greatest possible affection. He had caught her reading some of them and had said blandly: 'Safety in numbers, Sadie. It's when there's only one left that there's danger.'

'Danger?' she had asked.

'Of falling in love, Sadie.'

They had tea round the fire when the three of them got back and an early supper with the excuse that the sooner the children went to bed the sooner the morning when their presents would come. And when they were safely in bed, Sadie set about stuffing the presents into two old pillowcases, ready for Mr Trentham to tie on to the bedrails when he went to bed.

'I had no idea what I've been missing,' he observed, obediently picking up and packing the parcels away at her direction.

'But you must have had Christmas…'

'Not this kind of Christmas, Sadie. What time do you suppose those two will wake in the morning?'

'Very early indeed; it's the one morning in the year when no one's going to tell them to go back to sleep.'

'Luckily you're an early riser,' he pointed out dryly.

Sadie remembered that well when at six o'clock the next morning two small figures stole into her room, climbed into bed one each side of her, and began to open their presents in a state of excitement all the more intense for having to be quiet. All the same, the rustling of paper and the occasional badly suppressed squeal of delight sounded very loud to Sadie. Besides, the bed was crowded, for Tom had refused to budge before his usual getting up time and there wasn't an inch to spare.

Surprisingly there was. Mr Trentham, coming in with a tea tray, took in the situation at a glance, swept the presents which littered the bed on to the floor, boomed a genial Merry Christmas at every-one and sat down on the bed too. The children screamed with delight. 'Daddy, you never brought us tea when Miss Murch was with us,' declared Julie, and: 'Is it because you like Sadie?' asked Anna.

Unlike Sadie, who had gone very red in the face, Mr Trentham remained calm. 'That's telling, but one of the reasons is the frightful din of rustling paper which had been going on for hours.' He poured tea and handed it round, and without seem-ing to do so, took a good look at Sadie, sitting be-tween his daughters, her hair hanging round her shoulders, in her sensible pink winceyette nightie. Of course he knew that such garments existed, but he'd never seen one at close quarters before. There was no glamour about it, but he deduced that it would be nice and warm. He drank the tea, received

his daughters' thanks for the charming little wrist
watches he had given them and asked if Sadie had
opened her presents yet, and when she shook her
head, said: 'Well, go ahead, we all want to see what
you've got.'

The headscarf came first, wrapped in a great deal
of paper, and was duly admired, tried on and declared just the nicest scarf Sadie had ever seen. She
kissed each child in turn and opened her other parcels—hankies from Mrs Frobisher, more hankies
from Mrs Coffin, and a pair of knitted gloves from
Mrs Beamish. Sadie was trying them on when Mr
Trentham went out of the room and came back with
a large flat box. 'Happy Christmas, Sadie,' he said,
and laid it across her knees.

It was an extravagant box, tied with bright cords,
and when the lid was lifted, awash with tissue paper. Sadie pushed it gently aside to reveal amber
silk. She paused for a moment and looked at Mr
Trentham, comfortably settled on the bed again, and
he smiled and nodded his head. 'Go on, look at it.'

A crêpe-de-chine blouse and with it a matching
skirt; she had never had anything like it before in
her life. Its very simplicity spelt couture; its ele-
gance was indisputable. Just looking at it made her
feel beautiful.

'Oh, thank you—thank you, Mr Trentham! It's
so beautiful, I can't believe it!' She held up the

blouse against herself, hardly able to believe that it was hers. Dear kind Mr Trentham, giving her something so beautiful! She felt tears welling into her eyes and hung her head so that her face was hidden.

'Why are you crying?' asked Julie. 'Don't you like it? Sadie...?'

Sadie rubbed her cheeks with the back of her hand and put the blouse back carefully. 'I'm not crying,' she said in a wobbly voice. 'I've never had such a lovely dress before, you see, and I'm very happy—people cry a bit when they're very happy.'

'Oh, good,' said Julie. 'Well, kiss Daddy thank you, then.'

It was quite obviously expected of her. She leaned forward and kissed his cheek shyly and said, 'Thank you very much. Shall I wear it today?'

'Of course.' He looked so kind that she smiled widely at him and asked: 'Have you opened your presents, Mr Trentham?'

He fetched them from where they had been piled neatly on the landing. The socks were perfect, he declared, and the tie exactly what he wanted, he would wear both that very day. He opened Sadie's parcel without speaking and looked at the map for a long moment. 'You know my tastes, Sadie,' he said at length. 'Thank you. I shall hang it in front of my desk so that I can look at it constantly.'

She half expected him to kiss her since he had

kissed the two little girls, but he didn't, only smiled warmly, collected up the tea tray and with the remark that he wanted his breakfast in half an hour's time, went out of the room.

That night, in her bed, tired but very content, and with the new outfit on a coathanger on the wall so that she could feast her eyes on it, Sadie went over the day minute by minute. They had all gone to church in the morning, walking there because there had been a strong frost during the night and the snow was treacherous for a car. There had been almost the entire village there, and a great deal of laughing and talking as the congregation dispersed. Sadie, greeting all the people she knew, was cheered to hear Mr Trentham refusing invitations to drinks, to supper that evening, to lunch the next day, and although he hunted he refused to join the meet at Bridport on Boxing Day morning. Instead he invited quite a number of people for drinks on Boxing Night, casually mentioning it to Sadie as they walked home.

'How many are coming?' she asked, her mind already busy with sausage rolls and vol-au-vents.

'My dear girl, how should I know? I suppose about twenty—a few more?' He had turned to look at her. 'Anna and Julie can help carry round the food,' he suggested carelessly.

Just for a moment her mind boggled at producing

a variety of bits and pieces for so many people. And the glasses would have to be got out and polished. She frowned and he said with a touch of impatience: 'What are you frowning for? No frowns, today of all days.'

So she had put her small worries out of her head and smiled for the rest of the day; and it had been a success, she considered. The turkey had been tender and Mr Trentham had carved in a masterly fashion. The puddings had been pronounced first class and they had drunk claret and then port and cracked nuts, exactly as one should at Christmas. And in the afternoon the little girls had settled to undressing and dressing their dolls and Sadie, remembering, glowed with pleasure at Mr Trentham's real surprise that she had made all the clothes herself.

They had tea quite late and soon after the children went to bed Sadie had gone back to the sitting room and sat opposite Mr Trentham until it was time to go to bed herself. He hadn't noticed her, for he was absorbed in a book so she sat like a mouse, listening to the record player. Even when she said goodnight and thanked him for a lovely day, he barely answered her, although he had got up from his chair and opened the door and wished her a good night. But what else could she expect? She was only the housekeeper, wasn't she?

She crept downstairs very early the next morning, put a clean apron over her dressing gown, and began on the pastry for the sausage rolls. It would have to be puff pastry because she had the vol-au-vents to make too. She was arranging knobs of butter on her dough for the second time when the door opened silently and Mr Trentham came in.

'What the devil do you think you're doing?' he asked sourly.

'Good morning, Mr Trentham,' said Sadie politely. 'I'm making things for this evening—I won't have time during the day. I'll make you a cup of tea in a moment, but I'm afraid I must just see to this first or it will spoil.'

For answer he filled the kettle and put it on the stove. 'Sadie, I'm sorry, I had no idea—that's what comes of living in a house where you pick up the phone and order food for a drinks party and don't give it another thought. Can you manage? Is there anything I can do to help?'

Sadie, being Sadie, took him at his word. 'Yes, please. Will you take the sausages out of the fridge and put them on that chopping board. And when you've done that make the tea.'

When he had done that: 'What next?'

'It's a bit messy, I'd better do it.'

As she had hoped he said instantly: 'I'm quite able to do whatever it is.'

'There's a sharp knife in that drawer. Cut the skin off each sausage and divide it into four.'

To her surprise he did it very neatly, looking at her with a grin when he'd finished and saying: 'You didn't think I could, did you?'

She began to shape the sausage bits into tiny rolls. 'If I make eighty?' she asked him, and stopped to drink her tea.

An hour later they were ready on the baking trays for the oven, so were the vol-au-vents, as well as cheese straws, and Mr Trentham was making another pot of tea.

'There are olives,' said Sadie out loud to herself, 'and almonds and raisins and enough cream cheese to make stuffed celery…do you suppose that will do?'

He put another mug of tea into her hand. 'Superb, Sadie—it will be a roaring success. I'll take the children for a walk this morning and give you time to see to this lot.'

On his way out of the kitchen he turned to look at her. 'My God, how I've changed!' he told her.

Far more people came than he had told her. Sadie thanked heaven that she had made another batch of everything while he and the children had been out. The cottage bulged with gentry and villagers alike, and Sadie, so elegant in her new outfit that half her friends didn't recognise her, watched her food disappear and the glasses being filled and refilled again and again. Mr Trentham was an excellent host, but beyond him filling her glass from time to time, she hardly saw him.

That the whole thing was a success was a certainty. People started to leave reluctantly long after nine o'clock and the last few didn't go until almost an hour after that. As the door closed on them, Sadie whisked the little girls upstairs, whipped off their party dresses, popped them into their nighties and tucked them up. 'Baths in the morning,' she told them as she kissed them goodnight.

The chaos downstairs was almost more than she could face—glasses and plates and crumbs and paper serviettes screwed into balls, empty bottles in corners, and Tom voicing a loud protest because he hadn't had his supper.

Sadie put on an apron, fed him and took a tray to the living room. There was no sign of Mr Trentham; probably he couldn't face the mess, and she could hardly blame him. This, she told herself wearily as she collected glasses, was what he paid her for.

He came out of the dining room a few moments later and began to pick up the empties. 'If I were to suggest leaving this until the morning you'd sling something at me, I suppose?'

'Yes, I think I should. It won't take me long. It

was a lovely party.' She yawned and he smiled at her.

'A long day, Sadie. You looked charming.'

She paused to stare at him. 'Did I—did I really? I feel quite different in this dress…'

'You've been hiding your light under a bushel for too long, Sadie.' He paused at the door. 'Leave everything in the kitchen once you've tidied this place. I'll wash up—and that's an order. Oh, and by the way, we're all going up to Highgate tomorrow afternoon, but we'll talk about that in the morning. Now off to bed with you!'

He left her standing there, her mouth open with astonishment, bereft of words.

CHAPTER SIX

SADIE HAD GONE to bed with her head in a whirl.
How could Mr Trentham expect them to leave the
cottage at a moment's notice like that? A silly question, she admitted to herself. He did expect it, and
so they would get into the car and drive away at
exactly the time he had in mind. She sat up in bed
making a list of things to be done the next morning:
too many for one, so she went down the list allo-
cating tasks to the children and Mr Trentham. He
would probably be annoyed, but if he wanted to go
after lunch he would jolly well have to give a hand!

Having sorted things out to her satisfaction, she
went to sleep. She had prudently set her alarm for
half past six and by the time the others were awake
she had packed for herself, tidied the house downstairs, laid the table for breakfast and washed and
dressed. She told the little girls of their father's
plans as she helped them dress, and by the time
they sat down to breakfast they had been given their
small chores to do during the morning and were
agog to start. Mr Trentham, for once, came straight
to the sitting room. Presumably he had finished
whatever writing he was doing, or his muse wasn't

awake yet. His mood seemed genial enough, so Sadie got out her list. 'If you'd be kind enough to take Tom down to Mrs Coffin just before lunch,' she suggested as she filled his cup for a second time, 'and then call at Mrs Beamish's and ask her to stop the milk and the bread—oh, and get a form from the Post Office so that the letters can be forwarded...'

'Anything else?' asked Mr Trentham with a sarcasm she could have done without. And when she shook her head, 'And what will you be doing, Sadie?'

She chose to take his question seriously. 'Pack for the girls, store the food away, cover the potato clamp—it's not earthed up enough if we get some bad frosts—turn off the water, clean the fires and lay them ready for our return, get coffee, get lunch...'

He held up a large hand. 'All right, I asked for it! What about these two?'

'They're going to dust the whole house and then put out the clothes they'll need and the toys they want to take with them. Then they'll...'

'Enough! I see that you've got the slaves fully occupied. We'll leave at half past one.'

And they did! Sadie presented herself and the two little girls at one minute to the half hour, hatted and coated and ready to leave. Tom had been taken

to Mrs Coffin, all the messages had been delivered,
the cases packed, lunch eaten and cleared away and
the cottage as pristine as possible in the time she
had had. There had been no time to ask questions;
she had no idea for how long they were going and
Mr Trentham hadn't seen fit to tell her. The little
girls were put in the back of the car and she was
told to get in beside him, then off they went.

It was hardly a good day for driving; there had
been a hard frost again and the roads were treacherous, but Mr Trentham didn't appear to mind. He
drove fast but with more patience than she would
have credited him with, and after a little while she
sat back and enjoyed herself. Only as they ap-
proached London's suburbs did she lose some of
her content. Who would be at the Highgate house?
Was she expected to be housekeeper there as well?
Was she to be in sole charge of the children, and
what would they do with themselves all day? She
sat very quiet, her fine brows drawn together in a
thoughtful frown.

Mr Trentham, glancing sideways at her, smiled
to himself. 'I've not told you anything about my
home, have I, Sadie? It's run by Mrs Woodley and
her husband and there's a maid besides, Teresa.
They've been with me for a long time now, and I
think you'll like them. The house is quite close to
Hampstead Heath and I don't think you'll find it

too bad. The house is comfortable enough and
Highgate is a kind of village, not quite like Chelcombe perhaps, but still, in its way, charming. The
children have a few friends, not enough, I realise
that now. Miss Murch was too strict in many
ways—I had no idea that children could change so
much. My fault, of course, I thought that if I had
someone to look after them, dress and feed them,
that was enough.'

Sadie was shocked. 'But they are your children,'
she pointed out.

'Yes, but until they came to the cottage I saw
precious little of them. My fault.' She glanced at
him and saw how stern he looked; remembering
something unhappy in his past perhaps, missing his
dead wife. Perhaps that was why he hadn't been
able to love the children. And yet, in the last week
or so, he had seemed to enjoy their company. And
they certainly loved him, although Sadie had been
puzzled at their air of wariness when they were with
him—Miss Murch probably dinning into them that
they must never disturb him or take up his valuable
time. 'I expect we shall find heaps to do,' she told
him with an assurance which wasn't altogether gen-
uine.

They were there by teatime and Sadie, getting
out of the car in the quiet street with its row of tall
houses along one pavement and an enclosed garden

on the other, was agreeably surprised. Indeed Mr
Trentham had been right; it was charming, and the
house, three-storeyed Regency with ample gardens,
could have been in any quiet country town and not
the edge of London at all. Their welcome was just
as agreeable, with Woodley, short, stout and balding, opening the door to them and beaming at her
as well as the children, and Mrs Woodley, tall and
thin with a long sharp nose, and a severe expression, wasn't severe at all, but hugged the children
with real affection and greeted Sadie warmly.

'You'll be wanting to go to your rooms,' she said
in a motherly voice which sat strangely on her severe appearance. 'The children can run upstairs and
take off their hats and coats and I'll show you
where your room is, Miss Gillard.'

'Everyone calls me Sadie. I'm the housekeeper,
you know.'

'Then Miss Sadie, if you would prefer that.' A
motherly smile which matched her voice lit up the
severity.

They went up the stairs together; a charming
staircase built in a graceful curve against one wall,
leading to a small gallery above. Here Mrs Woodley turned down a corridor leading to the back of
the house.

'I've put you next to the children,' she explained.
'They'll like to know you're close by. That Miss

Murch slept on the floor above, she said they disturbed her in the mornings.' Sadie detected tartness in the pleasant voice. 'They're looking bonny, the pair of them—Mr Trentham said they'd come on a treat. Not that he saw much of them up here, Miss Murch saw to that.'

They had come to a halt outside a closed door at the end of the passage and before Mrs Woodley opened it, Sadie asked: 'Why, they're dear children.'

Her companion nodded. 'Indeed they are, Miss Sadie, and now they'll get the chance to be real children, bless them.' She opened the door. 'This is your room. If there's anything you need, just ask me or Woodley. The children are next door just up the passage, I expect you'll all come down for tea when you're ready.'

She smiled and nodded and went away, and a moment later a small brisk little person came in with Sadie's case. 'Teresa's the name,' she said cheerfully. 'If there's anything you want me to do, just say so.'

'Why, thank you, Teresa. I forgot to ask where the bathroom is.'

Teresa crossed the room and opened a door. 'And the little girls have got one of their own.' She whisked to the door. 'Nice to have you, miss,' she said, and nipped away.

Sadie went and sat on the edge of the bed and looked around her. The room was large—enormous if she compared it with the cottage—with a small bay window overlooking the back garden, a pretty stretch of green with flower borders and one or two ornamental trees and a high brick wall shutting away the neighbours on either side. Even on a cold winter's day it was pleasant. She turned away from it and looked at the room again. It was furnished with a small brass bed and white-painted furniture and there were two velvet-covered easy chairs, as well as a dear little writing desk in the window and a shelf of books. There were delicate china ornaments here and there and a bowl of hyacinths on the dressing table. Sadie hugged herself with delight and called, 'Come in,' as someone knocked on the door.

The children, bubbling over with excitement, both talking at once. 'Isn't it super that you're next to us? Miss Murch wouldn't stay in this room, whenever Daddy went away she moved upstairs— she said we were noisy. She wouldn't let us have a light either, Sadie. May we have just a teeny one, like we do at the cottage?'

'Why, of the course, and I'm here all night, you know. What a lovely room, isn't it? Is yours as nice?'

She was led away to inspect the room next door,

even larger than hers, delightfully furnished with small beds and pretty mahogany furniture. There was a small bathroom too and a large closet half full of clothes.

'My goodness, when do you wear all these?' asked Sadie.

'Almost never. Miss Murch bought things she liked for us and sent the bills to Daddy. She used to buy things for her too.'

'Well, one day when it's wet and we can't go out, you shall show me all your pretty things and try them on. Now what about faces and hands ready for tea?'

They took her downstairs to a small sitting room to one side of the hall. There was a cheerful fire burning and comfortable chairs and a big sofa drawn up before it. The room was restful, the curtains and carpet a warm honey colour, the chairs covered in green and amber chintz. Mr Trentham was sprawled in one of the chairs, staring at the fire, but he got up as they went in and asked them to sit down, then went to the door and shouted to Mrs Woodley for tea. Woodley brought it, with Teresa coming behind with a stand of plates of bread and butter and cakes. Just like a Hollywood film, thought Sadie, pouring tea at Mr Trentham's request.

She sat quietly, joining in the talk when she was

addressed but otherwise letting the children chatter and listening to Mr Trentham's deep voice answering them. She looked round her from time to time, seeing the splendid pictures on the walls and the china ornaments lying around. No wonder Miss Murch hadn't liked the cottage after living in a house such as this one!

'You like it?' Mr Trentham's voice broke into her musing.

'Very much. It's so peaceful too, not a bit what I expected.'

'It's peaceful now—the trouble is everyone knows where I live and the house is often far too full for my liking. Your room is comfortable?'

'Oh, it's lovely, I've never had such a lovely room...' Her words sounded inadequate to her own ears, heaven knew what they sounded like to him.

He nodded. 'Good. Don't let Julie and Anna annoy you.'

'But they never do.' Her voice was drowned in their squeaky protests.

'I'm glad to hear it. I've got tickets for *Cinderella* on Saturday evening—who wants to go?'

There were screams of delight from the children and a concerted rush to embrace him. His eyes met Sadie's over their heads. 'And you, Sadie, will you come with us?'

She smiled slowly, 'I'd love to', and added like a well brought up child, 'Thank you very much.'

'It's the evening performance—I'll leave you to arrange a meal, Sadie. I've an evening date, but I'll be back in time to drive you all to the theatre—it starts at eight o'clock. We'd better allow half an hour, I suppose—so be ready by about twenty past seven, will you?'

Her pleasure was a little dimmed, for it seemed as though he were giving up his own evening's pleasure in order to go with them, and that must have been the case, for he went on: 'I shall be out quite a bit while we're here, so I'll leave you and Mrs Woodley to sort out mealtimes. Feel free to take the children out, Sadie. The Savilles at the end of the road are bound to ask them round to tea one day, of course, and you'll go with them—they've got rather a nice au pair—you'll be glad to meet someone of your own age.'

She thanked him again and added in her sensible way: 'I'll go and unpack now. Would you like me to take the little girls with me?'

Before he could answer her, Woodley opened the door. 'Mrs Langley and Miss Thornton, sir,' he announced, and stood aside to allow two ladies to come in. They were elegant creatures, wrapped in furs and bringing with them a wave of scent. They swam towards Mr Trentham with shrill cries of,

'Darling, so you're back from that dump in the country!' before they kissed him and caught his arms, one on each side of him. They were pretty women, although not so very young, and Sadie envied them from the bottom of her heart.

Mr Trentham extricated himself gently. 'Julie, Anna, come and say hullo to Mrs Langley and Miss Thornton. And this is Sadie Gillard, my housekeeper.'

Two pairs of blue eyes looked her over, although neither of the ladies bothered to speak to her, let alone nod a greeting. Mr Trentham said impatiently: 'Take the children now, will you, Sadie?' and turned to his guests. 'Well, Eileen, how's the play going? Kay, did you enjoy the Bahamas?'

Definitely not my world, Sadie decided shooing the children before her back to their rooms to unpack.

Presently Teresa came to tell her that they would be having supper at seven o'clock and would she like hers with the children or later. The master would be out.

'Oh, with the children, please, Teresa. Are there any visitors downstairs or can we come down without disturbing anyone?'

'Master's in his study. The ladies have gone, Miss Sadie. But there's a playroom just across the gallery. There's a nice fire there too.'

'We'll go there, then. Do we have supper there too?'

'No, miss, that will be downstairs in the dining room. The master likes the children to eat properly.'

The playroom was cosy with well used furniture and great cupboards filled with toys. The children were getting tired, so Sadie settled by the fire, and told them to choose a book and she would read to them.

They brought her a rather battered copy of *Grimms' Fairy Tales* and took it in turns to choose a story. Anna decided on Faithful John, which Sadie found rather bloodthirsty. She much preferred Julie's choice—the beautiful poor girl sewing by her window and the prince riding by and the girl's needle going after him—absurd and impossible, but rather sweet.

'You sounded as though you would have liked to have been the beautiful young girl, Sadie,' said Mr Trentham from the door.

She hadn't heard him come in and none of them had seen him, as they sat bunched together on the elderly sofa. He was dressed to go out, tall and good-looking and assured; he would meet interesting people, she had no doubt, lovely girls with witty tongues, and he wouldn't get impatient or frown at them, because they were plain and wore sensible clothes. A great ache swamped her chest so that she

could hardly breathe. She would have given anything in the world to have been beautiful and clever,
so that Mr Trentham would take one look at her
and cancel his evening out and stay with her. Because that was what she wanted, only she hadn't
known it until that minute. She wanted him to fall
in love with her, because she'd fallen in love with
him. She might just as well wish for the moon.

She drew rather an unsteady breath and said the
first thing that came into her head. 'It's a charming
story, Mr Trentham—but most fairy stories are.'

He smiled with a hint of mockery. 'But it doesn't
do to believe them, Sadie.' He kissed the children
goodnight and nodded to her. 'Breakfast's at half
past eight, I'll see you then.'

Presently they went down to supper. At any other
time Sadie would have enjoyed the delicious meal
eaten in such elegant surroundings, but she had no
appetite. She was still getting over the shock of dis-
covering that she loved Mr Trentham, and not just
a girlish infatuation; she loved him just as much
when he was tiresome or impatient or ill-tempered,
she knew that she would still love him when he
was an old man, stomping round the house, bawling
everyone out. She wouldn't be able to stop loving
him. Even if he married again, it would make no
difference.

Julie and Anna chattered like magpies, but towards the end of the meal they became sleepy and made no objection when Sadie whisked them upstairs and into their beds, kissed them goodnight and tucked them up.

'You won't turn out the light, will you, Sadie?' asked Julie anxiously.

'No, love—look, I'll leave this little lamp on over here, and I'm going to leave your door just a tiny bit open so that if you want me in the night all you have to do is call me.'

She went to the door in a leisurely fashion, watched by the sleepy children. 'When you get a puppy, I daresay, if you ask daddy very nicely, he might let him sleep in a basket between your beds.'

'Miss Murch said dogs and cats are dirty, she wouldn't let us stroke them...'

'They're cleaner than we are—you watch Tom washing himself next time we're at the cottage. Goodnight, darlings, I'm coming to bed myself in no time at all.'

Mrs Woodley was waiting for her in the hall. 'I wondered if you'd like to see over the house, Miss Sadie, it's nice and quiet and it'll be nice for you if you know your way around.'

It would be a good way of spending an hour before she could decently go to bed and she had no wish to be by herself, because then she would think too much. 'I'd love it,' said Sadie at once.

'You've been in the small sitting room for tea,' began Mrs Woodley. 'This is the drawing room. The master doesn't use it all that much, only when he has company—it's a nice room; many's the party he's had here too.'

It was a lovely room, high-ceilinged and with a large bow window with window seats and elaborately draped curtains. The floor was polished wood almost covered by a thick carpet in pale pastel colours, and the chairs and two sofas were upholstered in the same pale colours. 'They dance here, too,' said Mrs Woodley. 'Mr Trentham's got a lot of friends.'

She crossed the room and opened a door in the farther wall. It gave on to a small room, comfortably furnished, at the back of the house, with french windows opening on to a conservatory which ran the width of the house at the back. 'And if we walk along here,' said Mrs Woodley, 'we come to the music room, so-called.' This was a smallish room with a grand piano and a pleasant arrangement of comfortable chairs and small tables. 'And the library,' and she led the way into another small room, lined with books, its polished floor covered with rugs and comfortable leather armchairs.

'It's a large house,' ventured Sadie, a little out of her depth.

'Well, a comfortable town house as houses go.

Here's Mr Trentham's study.' An austere room almost totally filled with a desk and chair and shelves of books and papers. 'The dining room you've seen. Now, upstairs. There's the master bedroom, not used and hasn't been for years, the master's bedroom, guest rooms...'

Mrs Woodley led the way upstairs and opened doors on to elegant rooms beautifully furnished and cared for. 'Then there's your room down this passage, and the children's room, and two more guest rooms. Upstairs there's our flat and Teresa's room and an ironing room, as well as two more bedrooms. We won't go there this evening, I daresay you're tired.'

Sadie said that yes, she was, and bed seemed a good idea. 'And thank you very much, Mrs Woodley, you've all been so kind.'

She went to sleep at once, although she had meant to stay awake for a little while and appreciate the luxury of fine linen sheets and a quilted silk eiderdown. It was gentle sobbing from the children's room which wakened her some hours later, a sobbing which got louder and wilder even as she got out of bed to listen. She didn't wait for a dressing gown or slippers but ran into the children's room, to find Julie sitting up in bed weeping uncontrollably.

Sadie sat down on the bed and took her in her

arms. 'There, there,' she said in her gentle voice. 'It's all right, just you tell Sadie what frightened you. Did you have a dream?'

It was difficult to hear the words being sobbed out so heartrendingly.

'She said she'd shut me in the cupboard if I told Daddy, and I started to tell him at breakfast and she stopped me and made him laugh,' Julie stopped to sniff and choke, 'and she put me in the cupboard and—locked the door!'

Two small arms were flung round Sadie's neck, almost throttling her. 'Don't let her come back, Sadie, will you? It was d-dark and no one came for ages, and she smacked Anna when she tried to let me out, and we didn't have our supper...' Another bout of sobs took over and Anna woke up, got out of bed and got on to Sadie's lap. 'I had blue spots on my arms,' she said, 'but she made me wear long sleeves so that Daddy wouldn't see.'

'What didn't Daddy see?' asked Mr Trentham softly, and came to lean over the end of his daughter's bed.

Which brought another flood of tears and a long, involved account from Anna. Her father listened silently, only coming to sit on the other side of the bed and take her on his knee. When she had at last finished and Julie's sobbing had dwindled into sniffs and long sighing breaths, he said: 'My dears,

this is all my fault, I should have...' he paused.
'Miss Murch seemed such a good governess, you
know, it wasn't until you came to the cottage that
I began to wonder. You must forgive me, it seems
to me that I need someone to look after me more
than you do. But Miss Murch is never coming back
again, and that's a promise, so you can forget her.
And now do you know what we're going to do?
We're all going to have a drink of nice hot cocoa
and then we'll go to bed, and tomorrow we'll think
of something exciting to do.'

He put Anna down and stood up. It couldn't be
all that late, thought Sadie, for he was still in his
evening clothes, which reminded her that she was
in her nightie, a very respectable garment, long-
sleeved and high-necked but still a nightie. She said
quickly: 'I'll get the cocoa. Mrs Woodley told me
where it was this evening just in case I should need
it.' She unwound Julie's arms from her neck. 'I
won't be long.' She kissed Julie's wet cheek and
padded to the door. Mr Trentham, watching her,
had a look in his eyes which hadn't been there for
a very long time, but she wasn't to know that. She
slipped into her room, put on her dressing gown
and slippers and went off to the kitchen.

The elaborate Cartel clock in the hall struck two
o'clock as she pushed open the baize door which
led to the kitchen and pantries. Just for a moment

she allowed her thoughts to dwell on Mr Trentham's evening, but she dismissed them at once; moping over impossibilities was a waste of time. She found the milk and the cocoa and put mugs on a tray and presently took it up to the children's bedroom where she found Mr Trentham still sitting on the bed with a child on each knee. Whatever he had been saying to them had made them extremely cheerful and giggly. They drank their cocoa and got back into their beds, demanding to be kissed and tucked in, and would Sadie please keep the light on in the passage just for a little while.

'We'll leave it on all night,' promised their father, and held the door for Sadie to go through. In the passage he took the tray from her. 'I'll see to that—go back to bed and go to sleep.' He started to say something else, but sighed instead and only added a goodnight, and that in a voice suddenly austere.

Over breakfast next morning he suggested a good brisk walk across Hampstead Heath. 'I've got to go out to lunch,' he observed, 'but we've time enough if we go as soon as we've finished breakfast.'

'In a bus?' demanded the children.

'Why not? We can walk there and take a bus back.'

It was a cold clear crisp day and Highgate Village looked decidedly pleasant. Sadie would have liked to have lingered to examine the charming houses and peer into the small shops, but Mr Trentham hurried them all along until they reached the Heath where, much to her astonishment, he proceeded to run races with his small daughters and when she stood uncertainly watching, caught her by the hand and whirled her away too. And presently, breathless and glowing, they all walked on, taking paths which he must have known very well indeed, for he never hesitated until they emerged at length on the other side of the Heath and caught a bus back. They had to go on top because of the children's urgent request to do so and sat squashed together on the back seat, with everyone pointing out various landmarks to her.

It had been a lovely morning, Sadie decided, combing small heads of hair and examining hands ready for lunch, only spoilt by the fact that Mr Trentham wasn't going to be home for lunch; indeed, as they reached the hall they could hear the Aston Martin racing away, too fast as usual. She wondered who he was so impatient to meet and wished, for the hundredth time, that she knew something about his work and his friends and what he did with his time when he wasn't bashing away at his typewriter.

She sighed so profoundly that Anna asked her if she was feeling quite well.

'Never better,' declared Sadie; after all, he'd be home for tea, or at worst dinner that evening.

But although he came home during the afternoon it was to go straight to his study where the phone rang non-stop until teatime, and then, just as Sadie had looked at the clock and decided that they might all go down to the sitting room for their tea, Teresa came to say that she would bring it up to the playroom because the master had visitors.

She passed him on the stairs later, as she was going down to fetch something from the kitchen. 'I'll say goodnight to the children now,' he told her as he paused beside her, half way up. 'I've told Mrs Woodley to serve your dinner after they're in bed; I daresay you'll enjoy that better. There's a good play on television, you might like to watch it.'

Sadie thanked him quietly, wished him a pleasant evening and went on downstairs. She was beginning to regret coming to Highgate: at the cottage she had mattered, even if it was only cooking his meals and running the house; here she was of no more importance than yesterday's newspapers. No wonder he needed somewhere quiet to write, for there was very little peace for him in London, but perhaps he had got bored when he wasn't actually working…

But the next day was Saturday and they were to go to the pantomime in the evening. They all

lunched together, then Sadie was dismissed kindly
enough afterwards and told to go and look at the
shops in the village for an hour while Mr Trentham
drove the children to Hampstead to see some
friends. So she helped the little girls into their coats
and hats, found their gloves and made sure that
their smart red shoes were clean, then sent them
downstairs to their father. When they had gone, she
put on her own coat and beret and set off to look
around her. Almost all the shops were shut for the
weekend, which was a blow, for she had some
money still and longed to spend some of it. She had
to content herself with a new lipstick and several
pairs of tights, and then, because it was too early
to go back to the house, she had a cup of coffee in
a small café which despite its chic interior, looked
forlorn because of its lack of customers. Saturday
afternoon was, after all, a time when families were
together at home, or out somewhere watching foot-
ball or visiting grandparents.

She walked back presently and reached the gate
just as the car drew up. She was immediately en-
gulfed in the two children tumbling round her, talking at once so that there was no need to do more
than give Mr Trentham a rather shy hello before
going indoors.

They were to have supper early and since Mr
Trentham was going out anyway, Sadie took the

children upstairs to have their baths and put on their best dresses. They had several of these, she discovered, a little shocked at the extravagant row of expensive little dresses hanging in the cupboard. They chose sapphire blue velvet outfits finally, and then, quite ready themselves, begged to go with Sadie while she got ready herself.

There was no difficulty in choosing what she was to wear; the blue wool and the amber crêpe hung side by side in an almost empty closet, and of course it would have to be the crêpe. She had a shower and got dressed while the children sat on the side of the bed, telling her about their afternoon. 'She's a widow lady,' explained Julie, 'and she's got a little boy a bit smaller than me, and a girl we don't like. We had to play in the nursery while she and Daddy had tea. They laughed a lot.'

Just right, thought Sadie unhappily, a widow with two children; she'd be beautiful, of course, and exquisitely dressed and good with children and giving dinner parties and going to the theatre. She got into the blue crêpe and immediately felt better, because there was no doubt that it did something for her. She brushed her hair back and tied it with a matching ribbon, made up her face in a rather inexperienced fashion, and pronounced herself ready. Blow Mr Trentham and his lovely ladies! She was going to enjoy her evening.

They were ready and waiting by the time Mr Trentham came to fetch them. The little girls had been too excited to eat much and Sadie hadn't wanted to eat at all, but she had done her best because of setting a good example. Now they got into the car, Mr Trentham having duly admired their dresses and pronounced all three of them very smart indeed, and Sadie went scarlet when Anna said: 'I think Sadie looks prettier than Mrs Wilcox, Daddy, don't you?' And luckily, not waiting for an answer: 'She uses very strong scent, but Sadie smells nice.'

Fortunately, Mr Trentham made no answer other than a grunt which could have meant anything.

They had splendid seats, the middle of the front row of the dress circle, so that they missed nothing of what was going on on the stage. Sadie, quite carried away by the splendour of the theatre and the magnificence of the costumes and scenery, sat between the two children, as rapt as they were. Mr Trentham had provided a box of chocolates for them and in the interval ordered ices for them, although he went off to the bar. It wasn't until the lights went up for the last time that Sadie had a chance to say how heavenly it had been. He was helping Julie into her coat and looked across at her, doing the same for Anna. 'I'm glad you enjoyed it, Sadie,' he said quietly. 'I found it heavenly too.'

It was getting on for eleven o'clock by the time

they got back. Sadie whisked the children upstairs
and into bed in no time at all, and was leaving the
room when Mr Trentham came in. He said goodnight to the sleepy little girls and followed Sadie
out into the passage.

'Are you hungry?' he asked her.

She was, although she hesitated to say so, not
that it mattered, because he didn't give her a chance
to reply. 'We'll go somewhere and have supper.
Teresa's watching the late night film, so the children will be all right. Where's your coat? Fetch it
and we'll go now.'

Sadie hadn't uttered a word and now she saw that
it would be useless to anyway. She got her coat and
followed him downstairs and out to the car and sat
without a word as they drove away. 'A pleasant
evening,' he observed blandly. 'Let's see if we can
make it still pleasanter.'

CHAPTER SEVEN

THEY WERE driving back the way they had come, back towards London's heart. After a few moments Sadie ventured: 'Isn't it a bit late for supper?'

Mr Trentham had been waiting for that. 'This isn't Chelcombe, Sadie, there are plenty of places open until the small hours.' And when she didn't answer! 'You're not tired?'

Of course she was tired, but she had no intention of saying so. She said primly: 'Since I've been at the Highgate house, I've not done anything to make me tired.'

'Good. We're going to Kettners. Have you heard of it?' and when she shook her head, 'They take their last orders at one o'clock in the morning.'

'How awful for the people in the kitchen,' said Sadie, and Mr Trentham laughed with the faint mockery she disliked so much.

'You and I see the world through different eyes, Sadie. If it comforts you at all, they get very good money. I hope it won't spoil your appetite.'

'No, I don't think so, I'm really quite hungry.'

She was glad of the amber crêpe as he ushered her into Kettner's restaurant. It was almost full and

they had to walk through a crowded room to reach
their table. Sadie walked to it behind the head
waiter, her head held high, her plain little face se-
rene, very anxious not to let Mr Trentham down.

The supper he had suggested wasn't quite what
she had envisaged. The menu was extensive and
written in French. She worked out one or two items
with inward shudders at the prices and then said in
her quiet way: 'Would you mind choosing for me,
Mr Trentham?'

He ordered smoked Scotch salmon with brown
bread and butter and lemon wedges, for them both,
and then crêpes de volaille Florentine for her and a
steak for himself. And when they had demolished
the salmon and the crêpes arrived said with relief:
'Oh, it's pancakes with a chicken filling and spin-
ach and cheese sauce.'

Mr Trentham agreed gravely and wished that the
chef could have heard her. The pudding she chose
for herself: Mont Blanc, a purée of chestnuts with
whipped cream which she consumed with childish
relish under Mr Trentham's amused gaze while he
toyed with a little Stilton.

He had laid himself out putting her at her ease,
talking about nothing in particular and making no
effort to persuade her to drink more than one glass
of the excellent hock he had chosen for her. She
had been a little surprised to find that he was drink-

ing a red wine while hers was white, but she had sense enough to know that the choice of wines was quite outside her province, nor had she any intention of asking him; she could get a book and read it up for herself.

Coffee was brought and over it Mr Trentham began to talk about more personal matters, and Sadie, nicely relaxed by the hock, was only too eager to listen.

'Sunday tomorrow,' said Mr Trentham. 'What about church?'

'Well, yes, I'd like to go if it's convenient.'

'We'll all go to St Paul's, the evening service.' He smiled at her.

'I'd like that very much, but are you sure...'

'Quite sure, Sadie. I thought that in the morning we might drive out to Pine Ridge Dogs' Home, to see if we can find a puppy for the children. They'll keep it for us until we go back to the cottage.'

'The children will love that. Couldn't we bring it back with us?'

'Well, I suppose so, you'll have extra work...'

'But I haven't any work,' she pointed out. 'I haven't done a thing since we came to Highgate.'

'You've looked after the children.' He put down his coffee cup. 'I feel guilty about them, Sadie. I thought that if they had a first class governess and everything they wanted, that that would be sufficient. I suppose that I wanted to forget the past and they were part of it. And now I begin to see what I've missed…'

She said, anxious to comfort him: 'You mustn't feel guilty, Mr Trentham. Miss Murch was clever, only the children knew what she was really like and she threatened them when they tried to tell you. You heard them the other night.'

'I should have listened to them, not dismissed the matter lightly as though it was just a childish fantasy. I'm not much use as a father, I'm afraid.'

She said bracingly: 'You will be if you practise hard enough!' She went pink. 'I'm sorry, I had no right to say that.'

He put down his coffee cup. 'You're almost too good to be true,' he observed, 'and much too good for me, Sadie.' His tone held mockery and the pink became red.

She said gruffly: 'I'm not good at all…'

He drank the brandy the waiter had brought him and lifted his hand for more, then continued just as though she hadn't spoken: 'A kind of nanny-cum-mother confessor. If I confess to you you won't tell anyone, will you?'

'Of course not, but I don't think you should talk like this to me, Mr Trentham—I'm only your housekeeper.'

'Ah, yes, but that's the crux of the matter. You're

not only my housekeeper, Sadie—and don't look at me in that enquiring manner, because I have no intention of explaining to you—not yet, anyhow.'

He leaned back in his chair for all the world as though he intended to sit there until breakfast time, and when she couldn't help giving a quick look at the clock on the further wall of the restaurant: 'Don't worry, they won't bring me the bill until I ask for it.'

It was half past one in the morning and she wanted to go to bed, but she guessed that even if she suggested that they should go home, Mr Trentham would ignore her. He wanted to talk and she would have to let him, for obviously he regarded her as someone in whom he could safely confide. She should be thankful for that, she reminded herself, even though he thought of her as a nanny. She poured herself another cup of coffee, black this time to keep her awake, and sat back quietly, her hands quiet in her lap.

'You don't wear any jewellery,' observed Mr Trentham, surprisingly.

'I haven't any.'

'I've never met anyone quite like you before,' he smiled briefly. 'The women I know spend a fortune on clothes and expect diamonds on their birthdays. I doubt if any of them would know how to stop a child crying and they certainly wouldn't get up in the night just for a few childish sobs.' Just for a moment mockery twisted his firm mouth. 'They wouldn't wear flannel nighties either.'

'Winceyette,' said Sadie in a clear voice.

'Is that what it's called? I don't think that my wife—Stella—would have known what it was. She had her things made to order by Janet Reger.' And at Sadie's questioning look: 'A very expensive designer of women's undies.' He lifted a finger and a waiter brought more coffee and Sadie poured a cup for them both. 'She liked only the best of everything. She didn't want children, but it was the done thing to have a son. I suppose that's why she didn't love Anna or Julie—oh, she was fond of them for half an hour a day, clean and sweet-smelling and with Nanny waiting to take them away the moment time was up.' He broke off. 'Do you hate me for telling you this?'

'No,' said Sadie. She was sitting motionless, but her feelings showed plain on her face. 'Only I don't quite understand…did you love the children…?'

Mr Trentham considered the matter at some length, going off into a brown study from which he emerged to say thoughtfully: 'I saw very little of them: my work took me away from home a good deal. Stella and I no longer loved each other and I think that prevented me loving Julie and Anna. The love was there, but it was somehow smothered. I doubt if you would understand that.'

'Why not? I'm not a halfwit.' She spoke so severely that he laughed.

'Do you know that I have a very poor opinion of women?' he asked her.

'Yes, you've made it plain from time to time. Mr Trentham, I think we should end this conversation, you're going to feel awful about it in the morning.'

'I haven't finished, and I never do things by halves.' He went on almost casually: 'Stella had a succession of boy-friends, you know. I did my best to understand at first—after all, I was away for weeks on end and she was young and very pretty and bored. Making a home and bringing up children were two things she couldn't stomach. In the end she left me—us. Anna was four and Julie was two and a half.' He drank the rest of his coffee. 'Woodley and Mrs Woodley and Teresa were wonderful; they coped until Miss Murch came along, and she seemed the answer to everything. Stella was killed soon after she left me—in a power boat joy-riding off the California coast. I find it difficult to lie to you, Sadie, so I won't tell you that I minded. I was sorry, in the way that anyone would be sorry to hear of the death of someone young and pretty, but that was all. Only a very few of my closer friends knew that she'd left me for good, and to escape the sympathy I didn't need I chose work that would keep me away from England for weeks, sometimes months. It was a mistake, I know that now. I should have stayed at home, but—I'm not making excuses—I didn't think that the children loved me.' He added in a suddenly harsh voice: 'Well, what have you to say to that?'

Sadie said calmly, 'The children adore you, and you've discovered what fun they are and love them too. I think that's the most important thing you've told me. I'm truly sorry about your wife—you've been lonely for years, haven't you? I know you've had your work and you're famous and I expect you've got quite a lot of money, but none of these are all that important, are they?' She stopped frowning. 'I expect I sound like a prig, but I don't mean to. Mr Trentham, I think you must marry again.' It cost her a lot to say that cheerfully. 'The children were talking about the lady you took them to have tea with—they seemed to think you might...'

His laugh was genuinely amused. 'Oh, my dear little Sadie, you mustn't believe all you hear. Pamela's the last woman on earth I would marry. No, I've ideas of my own.'

'I'm sorry—it's none of my business, but you did ask me...'

'So I did. What are we going to do about this in the morning?'

'I think it might be best if we forgot everything we've said, Mr Trentham.' She glanced at the clock: it was well after two now and one of the waiters was stifling a yawn, which made her want to yawn too. 'And thank you for bringing me out to supper; the food was lovely and it's a heavenly restaurant.'

'And the company, Sadie?' he was half smiling.

'There's been nothing wrong with your company, Mr Trentham.' She looked at him with her pretty dark eyes. 'You have been very kind giving me such a splendid treat.'

He lifted a hand and the waiter came with the bill, and presently they were in the car again, going back to Highgate. Neither of them said anything. Sadie wondered if Mr Trentham was regretting his evening. She hoped not. For her part, she would remember it for always; at least he liked her enough to talk to her as a person; she had always suspected that for most of the time he had thought of her as someone in the background who produced bacon and eggs when he wanted his breakfast and ironed his shirts.

The house was quiet as they went in, with only one lamp burning on the console table in the hall. Sadie went straight to the staircase with a quiet, 'Goodnight, Mr Trentham,' and was already half way up when he stopped her. She turned at the sound of her name and he came to the foot of the stairs and stood looking up at her. But after a moment he muttered: 'No, not now—go to bed,' and turned away and went into his study.

He was already at the breakfast table, deep in the Sunday papers, when she went down to breakfast with the children. He wished them all good morning, cautioned them to be ready by ten o'clock to go out and resumed his reading, but when the children had eaten most of their breakfast he put the papers down. 'Sadie and I decided last night that we might all go and choose a dog this morning,' he announced, and in the ensuing excitement, any awkwardness Sadie had been feeling went by the board.

It was a grey day but dry, and once at Pine Ridge, they spent an hour or so inspecting every dog there was. In the end they all agreed on Gladstone, no longer a puppy, who had been found wandering and half starved by the side of a motorway. He was rather on the large side and though mostly black labrador, his appearance hinted at a variety of ancestors. But he was liked by them all and, as Mr Trentham pointed out, would be less trouble for them to train than a puppy. He paid the sum asked of him, added a donation of a generous size and shepherded his party back to the car, with the little girls both holding Gladstone's lead.

In the car, driving back, he caught Sadie's eye as she turned round to look at the two children with the dog between them, on the back seat.

'I seem to have been missing a lot,' he said quietly, 'although probably I shall go berserk if that animal disturbs me while I'm working.'

She saw happily that he didn't mean a word of it.

Gladstone, after an initial inspection of his new home with the little girls as guides, settled down with a commendable aplomb, accepting the old travelling rug Mrs Woodley produced as his own, eating his meals tidily in the kitchen and returning to his rug after tea when he discovered that his new family were going out. 'And he'll still be here when we get back,' Sadie pointed out matter-of-factly when the children argued that they wanted to stay at home with him, 'but you don't often get the chance of going to church with your father.'

'And you?' asked Julie anxiously.

'And me,' Sadie smiled, and bent to kiss her.

The Cathedral was surprisingly full, and Sadie, used to the small church with its enthusiastic untrained choir, was a bit overawed. But the singing was sheer heaven and at the end of Evensong she got up and started to go reluctantly. While they were at Highgate she would contrive to come at least once more. They went out into the cold dark evening and bundled into the car and drove back through the almost empty streets to Gladstone, waiting patiently for them on his rug.

There was a slight contretemps when it was time for the children to go to bed. They wanted Gladstone to go to bed too, although Sadie pointed out that it was a little early for him: 'Besides, he'll have to go out for a quick walk later on.'

'But if he's with us, he'll look after us,' said Anna anxiously.

Sadie looked at Mr Trentham, pouring himself a drink and, she suspected, on his way to his study. They were his children and Gladstone was his dog; let him decide.

'Let's compromise. Let him stay downstairs until I've taken him for his walk, then he shall come upstairs and sleep in your room. That's a promise.'

And this they accepted without demur. Sadie saw them to bed, tucked them up and kissed them and hesitated about going downstairs again. Suppose Mr Trentham wanted to unburden himself again? Suppose, which was worse, he regretted the previous evening? On the other hand, if she didn't go down exactly as she always did, he might think that she had attached more importance to their talk than he would wish. She went downstairs, very slowly.

There was no sign of him. She went to the small sitting room and got out the knitting she had start-

ed—gloves for the children—and it was all of half
an hour before Woodley, coming to make sure that
the fire was burning well, informed her that Mr
Trentham had gone out. 'Some party or other,
miss—the master is much in demand socially.' He
sounded faintly disapproving.

'I expect so,' said Sadie in a disinterested way.
'And there's no need to make the fire up for me,
Woodley, I think I'll go to bed; it's been quite a
full day.' She looked at the dozing Gladstone. 'I'll
take him round the square and settle him with the
children as their father promised. I'd better leave a
note, hadn't I?'

Woodley agreed gravely. 'A nice quiet dog, Miss
Sadie, and very good for the children. There's paper
and pen in the little desk under the window.'

She wrote her note, got her coat and attached
Gladstone to his lead. It was a clear frosty night
now and she marched briskly up one side and down
the other side with the obedient Gladstone trotting
beside her. Back inside, Woodley was waiting to
open the door and wordlessly proffered a towel for
the dog's paws. Sadie, taking it gratefully, pondered
the fact that it took no time at all to get into the
habit of being waited on, and with pleasantness too.
In a week or two she'd be back at the cottage, peeling potatoes and scrubbing the sink.

It was the very next day, when Mr Trentham appeared suddenly in the middle of lunch, he informed them that he was going away for a brief holiday. 'A week—ten days, I'm not sure. The Greek Islands, I think. I've some thinking to do.' He glanced briefly at Sadie. 'You'll be all right? No point in leaving an address—I'll probaby ring you anyway.'

Sadie nodded just as she had done on the other occasions when he had asked her the same question.

'Are you going by yourself, Daddy?' asked Anna, and when he said yes, Sadie felt a surge of relief. It didn't last long, though; probably he was joining someone on some idyllic island where they would laze in the sun all day and dance half the night...

Mr Trentham asked curtly: 'You don't look very happy about it, Sadie?'

She came back to reality with a bump. She said primly: 'On the contrary, Mr Trentham, I'm perfectly happy, thank you.'

'May we have a party, a teeny-weeny one, while you're away, Daddy?' asked Julie. She smiled enchantingly at him and he smiled back.

'I don't see why not, if Sadie doesn't mind.' He lifted an eyebrow at Sadie, who said promptly:

'What a lovely idea—we'll write the invitations today and ask Mrs Woodley to make some cakes.'

'And have games and make a noise?' asked Julie hopefully.

'Well, as it's a party I daresay we shall do that too,' said Sadie. 'When shall we have it?'

The discussion became lively and Sadie, peeping at Mr Trentham, thought that he looked a little forlorn. She wanted to comfort him, tell him that they would miss him, and did he really have to go? but she squashed all that. After all, he was able to make his own decisions and do exactly what he liked, and if he chose to go away and leave his children while he wallowed on some magical beach that was his own business. She said cheerfully: 'Well, let's go and make that list and then go and see Mrs Woodley. Perhaps she'll let us go shopping for her.'

It was Julie who asked: 'When are you going away, Daddy?'

'This afternoon, love.'

'Oh, then we'll say goodbye now, shall we? We're going to be busy.'

By the time they had got back from the shops with Mrs Woodley's list of jellies and almonds and icing sugar and extra eggs, he had gone. It was silly to feel sorry for him, Sadie told herself. If she could see him now, boarding a plane with a host of friends, exchanging clever small talk with not a care in the world, she would see how wasted her feelings for him were and what a waste of time it was loving

him, only surely that was never a waste. She sighed
deeply and then, because it was no good crying for
the moon, she fetched the invitations she had written at the children's dictation, put Gladstone's lead
on, and went along to the post.

The party was for three days' time and since the
children hadn't many friends and they all lived
close by, there was no reason for any of them to
refuse. Sadie, in the kitchen helping Mrs Woodley
decorate the trifles, was glad to have something to
do; she was missing Mr Trentham very much indeed; it was like walking round with an empty
space inside you, and no amount of common sense
could make it feel any different. Presently she went
along to help the little girls into their party dresses
and then got into her blue dress; the first little guests
would be arriving at any minute.

The party was a success, although it wasn't
the sort of party Sadie would have had for her
own children. She didn't consider that the row of
nannies sitting round the drawing room wall made
any contribution to its success, nor did she think
that the children had enough friends—indeed, she
wasn't at all sure that they were real friends, and
they certainly didn't enjoy themselves like the children at the Christmas party at Chelcombe. All the
same, the little girls were delighted with the whole

affair, talking about it endlessly while they had their
supper and she got them ready for bed.

'That silly Lucy Price,' said Anna, 'she kept saying that she didn't feel well, she sicked up her trifle
and her nanny was furious!' She added smugly:
'I'm always well, aren't I, Sadie?'

But she didn't want her breakfast in the morning
and when Sadie took her temperature, it was over
a hundred. 'I don't feel well,' said poor Anna, and
burst into tears against Sadie's comforting shoulder.

Sadie put her back to bed, gave Julie her painting
book and paints in the playroom and went to con-
sult with Mrs Woodley. 'There was a little girl who
was ill at the party, Anna mentioned it last night—
Lucy Price. I wondered if I telephoned to see if
she's started something. And it would be kind, if
it's not an awful nuisance, if someone could take
Gladstone for a quick walk?'

Woodley obliged with his usual dignity and Sadie went off to phone. Lucy had 'flu, said Nanny
at the other end, and they'd had the doctor and Sadie had better get him too. There was a lot of 'flu
about, went on the voice, as though that helped the
matter.

Sadie phoned the doctor, consulted with Mrs
Woodley again and when that gentleman came ac-
companied him upstairs to Anna's bed. Doctor
Rogers was tall and thin and inclined to be pom-

pous, and he quite evidently didn't think much of
Sadie. 'The housekeeper, are you?' he commented,
'Well, I suppose you can cope with some simple
nursing. The child's poorly, but she'll pick up once
the antibiotic starts working. Keep her in bed and
give her a light diet.' He looked at her curiously.
'Where is Mr Trentham?'

'Abroad.'

'Ah, well, there's no need to bother him at the
moment.' He bade her a rather distant good day and
went downstairs where Woodley was waiting to let
him out.

He had said that the antibiotics would take a little
time to work, and in the meantime Anna got worse.
Sadie thanked heaven for the kind Woodleys, and
Teresa took over Julie and Gladstone and left her
free to nurse the child, who became more restless
as the day wore on and by nightfall had a high
fever. Julie was moved to another bedroom close
by with Gladstone for company and Sadie prepared
for a long night. Round about four o'clock in the
morning, Anna fell asleep, and Sadie, still sitting in
the chair she had drawn up near the bed, went to
sleep too.

She woke when Anna did, gave her a drink,
washed her hot face and hands and put her into a
clean nightie, then gave her another drink and her

medicine. Her temperature was lower, perhaps the antibiotic was already doing its good work.

But as the day wore on, Sadie saw that although Anna was a little better, she was by no means on the mend yet. There would be another bad night, possibly two. She had had her meals on a tray in the playroom and Julie had eaten in the kitchen with the Woodleys and Teresa in the hope that she wouldn't get 'flu as well. Sadie, trying to make Anna comfortable for the night, wished with all her heart that Mr Trentham would phone. He didn't, of course. She spent another almost sleepless night again, although in the morning it was obvious that Anna was better.

With a child's resilience she demanded food, and when she wasn't eating she was sleeping. Sadie thanked heaven silently and caught up with her own sleep as best she could, taking catnaps whenever Anna did. Julie was still being looked after by the Woodleys, and it was during the afternoon that Woodley came upstairs to see Sadie. He had just been out with Gladstone and came to tell her that Mrs Woodley wasn't quite happy about Julie. She was looking hot and flushed and was off her food.

Sadie pushed back the hair she had been longing to wash for two days now. 'Oh, Woodley, has she got 'flu now, do you suppose? I'll get Doctor Rogers again...'

He came within the hour, pronounced in a pompous what-can-you expect voice that Julie had 'flu, handed over another lot of antibiotics, assured Sadie that Anna was progressing nicely, and took himself off.

He had looked at Sadie's tired white face as she accompanied him down to the hall, and thought what a very plain girl she was. Which was true enough. She hardly looked her best with the prospect of another broken night which depressed her very much.

She had put Julie to bed in her own shared room with Anna and once she had settled her, she fetched Teresa to sit with the two of them while she showered and got into her nightie and dressing gown, had a hurried meal and took over again. Julie was querulous and Sadie had a nasty feeling that she was going to be a bad patient. And she was right. The child refused to lie down, to drink the barley water she was offered, to stop crying… Sadie, fortified by the hot coffee and sandwiches Mrs Woodley had provided, read one story after another, the words dancing hazily before her heavy eyes, her tongue tying itself into knots. The one blessing was that Anna, with all the resilience of youth, was sleeping peacefully.

About two o'clock, Julie at last fell asleep, and Sadie seized the chance to go to the kitchen and fetch more cold drinks. One light had been left on in the hall; she crept down in the dimness, jug in hand, and was half way across the hall when a sound at the front door made her stop dead.

It was a very small sound, but at that hour of the night it scared her stiff. She gripped the jug tightly in both hands and watched the door.

It opened and Mr Trentham walked in.

CHAPTER EIGHT

THE WAVE OF relief and delight which swept over Sadie at the sight of him took all the colour, and that wasn't much, from her face and made her dizzy. It was instantly replaced by quite irrational fury.

'Where have you been?' she hissed at him. 'You're never home when you're wanted!'

Mr Trentham had shut the door and was leaning against it, watching her. His brows rose and he half smiled. 'Well, well,' he said gently, 'what a welcome home! You sound like a loving wife and you look...' he stopped and stared hard at her. 'You look frightful. What's happened?'

To be told she was looking frightful, however true it was, was the last straw on the camel's back; two large tears rolled down Sadie's cheeks. But crying got you nowhere; she wiped them away with the back of her hand, steadied her voice and said: 'Julie and Anna have got 'flu. Anna's getting better, but Julie is feverish and not very well.'

Mr Trentham crossed the hall in a couple of long strides, took the jug from her and put a large hand on her shoulder. 'Oh, my poor little Sadie! You've had no sleep, no rest, probably no food—you're exhausted!'

'No, just tired. Mrs Woodley has been marvellous, so has Teresa, and Woodley has been looking after Gladstone…I must get some more lemonade, the children get thirsty. Do you want anything to eat or drink, Mr Trentham?'

'No, and if I did you certainly wouldn't be allowed to get it. Fetch the lemonade; I'll come up with you.'

He threw off his coat and put his case down in the hall and when she came back, walked upstairs with her to the children's room. They were sleeping still, but Julie was restless and flushed.

Mr Trentham put the jug down on a table. 'Now tell me exactly what has to be done,' he commanded in a quiet voice, 'and then you'll go to bed. And no arguing, please. If you don't go quietly I shall pick you up and carry you there.'

He meant it. Sadie said: 'Very well, thank you, but I should like to get up about seven o'clock so that I can see to them both.' And when he nodded: 'This is what you have to do…' It wasn't much; giving drinks, shaking pillows, bathing a too warm little face and hands, soothing…

He nodded. 'OK—off you go,' and she went thankfully to bed, too tired to feel unhappy because he thought she looked frightful.

She slept soundly until her alarm clock woke her, and when she went to the children's room it was to find Anna sleeping quietly and Julie curled up in her father's arms. They were both asleep too. Sadie silently made the bed, went to the kitchen where she found Teresa making tea, filled the lemonade jug once more, and bore it, together with tea for two, back to the children's room. Anna stirred as she went in and Sadie took her temperature, gave her a drink and went to run her bath, thankful that at least one child was normal again. She wrapped Anna in her dressing gown and sat her on a chair while she made the bed, and then, since the other two showed no sign of waking, bathed her and popped her back into bed. The tea would be cooling by now; she poured herself a cup and sat down on the edge of Julie's bed to drink it, but only for a moment. Mr Trentham opened his eyes, yawned hugely and asked in a carrying whisper: 'Tea?'

He looked worn out, with a night's growth of beard and bags under his eyes and his hair going in all directions; Sadie had never loved him so much. She poured his tea and took it to him and he cradled Julie carefully in one arm to take it. 'You've slept?' he asked.

'Very well, thank you, Mr Trentham. Anna's much better, almost well in fact, and I fancy that when Julie wakes she'll be feeling more herself.'

She heard her voice, very prim, very cool, exactly opposite to what she was feeling.

'Still angry with me, Sadie?' he asked lazily.

'No, Mr Trentham. I—I—was tired. I'm sorry if I was rude.'

'And yet, when you saw me, you looked...over the moon.' He held out his cup for more tea. 'I wonder why?'

She said stiffly: 'Naturally I was glad to see someone.'

'I'm disappointed. I hoped you were glad to see me.' He drank his tea, and as Julie stirred: 'Will you see to her now? Anna's asleep.'

'She's been awake, I gave her a bath and popped her back in bed.'

He put the half-asleep Julie in her arms. 'Do I see you at breakfast?' he wanted to know.

'It rather depends on how Julie is.'

He nodded and got up and Sadie asked hesitantly: 'Did you have a good holiday?'

With his hand on the door handle he turned to look at her. 'No,' he said, 'I did not. The sensible thoughts I should have had were very completely obscured by daydreams.' His fine mouth turned down at its corners. 'At my age too! I even found myself quoting poetry. You know Robert Herrick?' and before she could nod a little uncertainly, 'He wrote ''How love came in, I do not know''—well,

I don't know either. My peaceful, hardworking life has been shattered, and I find that I have no interest in anything.'

Anna had wakened up and was sitting up in bed, listening. 'Why don't you stop working, Daddy, and go out every evening with a pretty lady? I s'pect she'd be interesting.'

He smiled at her but he looked longest at Sadie. 'That might be an idea. Who shall I start with?'

'Sadie, of course.'

Sadie bent over the tray and no one could see her face. 'No, love, that wouldn't do; I'm not pretty and I'm not a lady. I'm sure you can think of someone else.'

'You're not a bit pretty, but your eyes smile,' said Anna, 'but I see what you mean. There's Miss Thornton and Mrs Wilcox, though she's rather old.'

'But very handsome,' suggested her father softly, his eyes still on Sadie. 'I think I must take your advice, Anna.' He smiled slowly. 'What do you think, Sadie?'

'Since you didn't enjoy your holiday, Mr Trentham, I should think it might be a good idea to— renew your friendships.' She made herself look at him then, presenting him with a politely interested face which gave away nothing of her feelings.

He said blandly: 'I shall take your very sound advice, Sadie. That is if you promise not to meet me on the stairs every night and demand to know where I've been.' And when she prudently held her tongue: 'Would you like help with the children? Shouldn't Doctor Rogers come again?'

'I can manage very well, thank you, but I would like the doctor to come and advise me how long they should remain indoors.'

He nodded. 'I'll arrange that. Anna seems quite well again.' He grinned at the child as he spoke. 'And Julie is on the mend, I hope.'

Thank heaven they had recovered so quickly, thought Sadie, although they weren't out of the wood yet. There would be a few days' convalescence and both children would be peevish and bored. She foresaw endless games of Ludo and Scrabble and herself hoarse from reading Hans Andersen's fairy tales. But they were dear children and she was fond of them, and once they could go out again she would plan one or two outings. She took Julie's temperature, wondering when they would be going back to the cottage. No one had mentioned it, but of course. The children wouldn't be going to school for another ten days and she was quite prepared for Mr Trentham's habit of waiting until the last minute before telling her anything.

Julie's fever was much less and she showed some interest in her breakfast. Sadie washed her and sat her up in bed, bade Anna keep an eye on her and went away to have her bath and dress. She was on the point of going down to the kitchen to get their trays when Teresa appeared.

'Morning, Miss Sadie,' she beamed at the little girls. 'Better, aren't they—isn't that nice now? The master says you're to go to breakfast and I'll bring up the trays.'

'But, Teresa, I don't suppose you've had your breakfast yet…'

'Yes, I have, miss. I'll stay with these two while they eat.'

'Well, thank you, Teresa, you're kind. I shan't be long.'

'You eat a good breakfast, miss. You had a bad night, so I'm told—you should have called us.'

'I expect I should have, only Mr Trentham came home as I was going to the kitchen. He was kind enough to stay with the children and I had a good sleep.'

Mr Trentham was already at the table when Sadie reached the dining room. He got up and pulled out a chair for her, wished her good morning, asked Woodley to bring some fresh toast and excused himself for continuing to read his post. His manner was pleasant, but he sounded absentminded.

Sadie ate her breakfast in silence and as quickly as she was able; she quite appreciated that Mr Trentham had a large post to read, but surely he could have spared a word or two? As it was every swallow and every crunching bite into her toast sounded like thunder in the awful quiet. She could have eaten more, for although she was a small girl and still too thin, she had a healthy appetite, but she got up from the table as soon as she decently could, murmured her excuses and made for the door. She had taken two steps when Mr Trentham raised his head.

'Why are you whispering?' he wanted to know.

She stood still, half turned towards him. 'I'm not. You didn't look as though you wanted to be disturbed.'

'I am already disturbed, Sadie.' A remark which meant nothing to her. 'Will you sit down again for five minutes?' he added, to her great surprise. 'Please.'

She sat composedly and looked at him. No one would have guessed that he had spent the night in a chair with a small girl on his knees. He looked well rested, well groomed and wore the smilingly bland expression which she never quite knew how to take.

'As soon as the children are quite better, I think a day at my sister's might be a good idea—you'll come too, of course. She lives at Maidenhead. And a day at the Tower, perhaps? Don't look so astonished, Sadie, it's the done thing to take your young there. They love dungeons and suchlike horrors at their age.' He paused to think. 'I wonder if they've been on a bus tour of London? We might do that as well. When does school start at Chelcombe?'

'I'm not quite sure, but I believe it's about the sixteenth.'

'Good—what with escorting the three of you during the day and wining and dining the pretty ladies thrust upon me so ruthlessly by my daughter, I imagine I shall have no time for daydreams. Do you have daydreams, Sadie?'

She said quietly: 'Oh, yes, Mr Trentham, I should think most people do.'

'And what are yours, I wonder? To marry a millionaire and live happily ever after.'

She said even more quietly: 'Just to live happily ever after.'

'Money doesn't appeal to you?' He was laughing at her.

'Of course it does, but it's not much use...I mean, what would be the use of marrying a millionaire if you didn't love him?'

'What—you'd rather have a flask of wine, a loaf of bread and thou, than an unlimited dress allowance?'

'Well, of course I would.' She was suddenly impatient with him. 'Was there anything else you wanted to talk about, Mr Trentham?'

He sighed. 'A great many things, Sadie, but not now. I'll bring Doctor Rogers up when he comes.'

She escaped with something like relief.

Anna was sitting up in bed, demanding to get up, and Julie was well enough to listen to the story Sadie was reading by the time Doctor Rogers arrived. Anna was pronounced well, although she was to stay in the house for another day, and Julie, with a normal temperature now, could get up on the following day provided she had no more fever. The two men went away and Sadie helped Anna dress; before she had finished Mr Trentham was back again. 'I'll have Anna with me,' he offered, and frowned a little at Sadie's surprise. 'She can do a jigsaw or draw in the study while I write some letters.' He added tetchily: 'You have no need to look like that, Sadie, I'm quite capable of looking after my daughter.'

He had gone, with Anna prancing along beside him, before she could utter a word.

And Anna stayed with him for the rest of the day. It wasn't until her bedtime that she finally came upstairs, full of the things she had done and what she would do on the next day and the jigsaw she had almost managed to finish. Sadie got her ready for bed, fetched Julie's supper and presently, with both little girls asleep, went downstairs herself.

Just in time to see Mr Trentham getting into his

coat in the hall. He was wearing a dinner jacket and when he saw her, he called out: 'I think I've earned an evening out, don't you, Sadie?'

She was tired and dispirited, but she answered him cheerfully. 'Indeed you have, Mr Trentham; I hope she's a very pretty lady.'

He crossed the hall to her and to her great surprise, bent down and kissed her. 'I'm out of practice,' he told her airily. 'That's by way of a rehearsal.'

She stood quite still until he had gone out of the house, then she went to her supper. Mrs Woodley had cooked a delicious meal, but Sadie didn't really notice what she was eating. She felt as though her heart was breaking—but that, of course, was nonsense. Hearts didn't break, they might crack a little, but cracks could be mended.

She didn't see Mr Trentham at all during the following day. She heard his voice in the hall as she helped the little girls get dressed, but there was no sign of him at breakfast; away all day, Woodley told her, and only back in the evening for an hour to change his clothes for some dinner or other. So the three of them repaired to the playroom and passed the day happily enough, on the little girls' part at any rate, in painting and making plasticine models and playing with Gladstone. After lunch, Sadie, longing for a breath of air, got Teresa to sit with the children while she put on her coat and took the dog for a walk. It was another grey cold day, but it was dry, and she stepped out briskly with Gladstone striding out beside her. She walked for half an hour and then turned for home, feeling better, telling herself that self-pity would get her nowhere. She arrived back at the house with glowing cheeks, took Gladstone down to the kitchen for his tea, and went back to the playroom.

She heard Mr Trentham come in presently just as the three of them, greatly hindered by Gladstone, were finishing a jigsaw. They were on the floor before the fire and Sadie didn't get up as the children ran to meet their father. Instead she busied herself collecting up the pieces and putting them back in their box. She had said good evening pleasantly, but that was all. He looked tired again and in no mood for small talk, and she was surprised when he asked: 'Do you think the children are well enough to go to Maidenhead tomorrow?'

There were screams of delight. 'Yes, I think so. If I wrap them up warmly and they don't get tired— I mean, a long day...'

'It won't be a long day, you forget, I have to be home to change for the pretty lady.' He gave her a mocking smile and when Julie asked: 'Is she very pretty, Daddy?' answered: 'Absolutely stunning, love.'

'Prettier than the one you're going out with this evening?'

'Oh, definitely.'

'It's not Mrs Langley? She laughs so loud.'

'No, it's Miss Thornton, she hardly laughs at all, but she's on a diet, so I expect that makes her sad.'

'What sort of a diet?'

'Lettuce leaves and yogurt to keep her a lovely shape.' He swung the child up in the air, kissed her soundly, did the same for Anna, bade a casual goodnight to Sadie and went away. He came back almost at once.

'We'll go directly after breakfast,' he said, and went out again.

It was a lovely morning, frosty and cold sunshine and a pale blue sky. The little girls, well wrapped up with Gladstone panting happily across their feet, were packed into the back of the car, Sadie, in her tweed coat and the blue wool dress, was told briskly to get in beside Mr Trentham and they were off. The rush hour was almost over and the mid-morning traffic was only just starting. Mr Trentham drove south to Hammersmith, got on to the M4 and raced along it to Maidenhead, turning off through Bray before he reached the town. Lady Crawley lived on the other side of the village in a large, rambling house set in a small park. It looked comfortable and lived in, a supposition borne out by the opening of a side door and the emergence of three children and two large dogs, followed by their mother, walking with unhurried dignity.

Mr Trentham had got out, opened the door and allowed his children and Gladstone to meet the on-coming pack, and then gone round to Sadie's side and ushered her out too. His sister had reached them by now, smiling and sailing through children and dogs with unruffled calm.

She embraced her brother and turned to Sadie, who was feeling shy, and put a friendly arm through hers. 'Nice to see you,' she told her. 'You must be feeling like chewed string! 'Flu's ghastly at the best of times, combine it with small children and it's beyond words. Come on in and have coffee. The children will be all right for a bit. Nanny's coming down in a moment; she'll see that they get their cocoa and look after them until lunch.'

She slipped an arm in her brother's and the three of them walked into the house, using the side door. It opened on to a stone-floored passage, full of clob-ber; wellingtons, fishing rods, old tennis shoes and racquets, a cricket bat or two, raincoats hung on pegs, dog leads, and where it opened into a small carpeted lobby, a basket with a cat and kittens.

'Tabitha's been at it again, I see,' said Mr Tren-tham idly as they all paused to admire the little creatures. 'I'll have one of them—Mrs Woodley fancies a cat about the house. We'd better have two, then they'll be company for each other.' They went on through a door on the other side of the lobby and came into a square hall, panelled and rather dark, and so into a pleasant room, handsomely furnished but rather untidy. Lady Crawley swept a pile of magazines off a chair and invited Sadie to sit down.

'Take her coat,' she commanded her brother, 'and put it in the hall and ask Maria to bring the coffee, will you?' She sat down herself near Sadie. 'My husband's at his office this morning, but he'll be back after lunch. I'd like him to meet you,' and then: 'What do you think of Oliver?'

Sadie hadn't expected that. She went very red and repeated: 'Oliver?' in a parrotlike voice. 'Mr Trentham…he's—well, he's…'

'Difficult, bossy, moody, bad-tempered—I know, but he's quite a darling really.' She eyed Sadie, who felt like something under a microscope. 'You've discovered all that for yourself.' It was a statement, not a question, and Sadie said with a touch of defiance: 'Yes, I have.'

Her companion had no intention of letting the matter rest there; luckily Mr Trentham and the coffee arrived and his sister said at once: 'Come and tell me about your holiday. Was it a success?'

'If you mean did I achieve peace and quiet—no,

it was an utter failure; on the other hand, I had my mind made up for me.'

She smiled at him. 'You'll try your luck?'

He nodded and went on pleasantly: 'Nanny's fetched the children inside—the dogs too. They've gone up to the nursery, she's got her hands full.'

Sadie put down her coffee cup. 'Perhaps I could help...' she began.

Mr Trentham said sternly: 'Certainly not! It's your day off, more or less, I must owe you a week of them at least. Besides, this is a heavensent opportunity to discuss the party.'

Sadie just managed not to ask: 'What party?' and was glad that she hadn't when he went on: 'I'll make it informal, I think, don't you? Buffet supper—dancing—I owe a great many evenings out, so I'll ask them all and get them dealt with at the same time. There'll be about fifty, I should think. You'll come, my dear?'

'Of course. Are we to dress up?'

He shrugged. 'I can't imagine any of the girls turning up in woollen dresses!' His eyes fell on Sadie, who had gone scarlet and he said at once: 'Sadie dear, I had no intention—forgive me, you look charming in that dress. I mean no unkindness to you, of all people.' He crossed to her chair and picked up her hand and kissed it gently. 'You look nice in a sack,' he finished, and smiled at her so that her heart turned over.

His sister regarded them with smiling eyes. 'Sadie should wear taffeta.' She frowned in thought. 'Something rich—I know, a dark green. Don't whatever you do, buy something demure and grey.' And seeing Sadie's mouth opening to protest: 'And don't tell me you aren't going to get a dress—of course you are. There's a very good boutique in Highgate Village, they're bound to have something. Oliver, see that she goes there.'

'I will.' He had gone back to his chair, and Sadie, her cheeks cooling, asked, 'When is the party to be?'

He grinned at her. 'Well, I've several more pretty ladies—five days from now? I'll do some phoning this evening.'

'Pretty ladies?' asked his sister.

'Ah yes, my daughters and Sadie seem to think that I might take more interest in things if I were to go out more often with pretty ladies. I've got through three so far.'

'And not, I hope, raised their hopes,' said his sister severely.

The children joined them for lunch. They were nicely behaved but chatty, so that conversation between the grown-ups was scanty, and after lunch they all put on hats and coats and went outside to inspect some trees that had just been planted, the three dogs trailing them. Presently they were joined by the master of the house, who kissed the children, his wife and Sadie, shook hands with his brother-in-law and asked if it was time for tea. They went back to the house then, and Sadie found herself walking with him, completely at ease because he was so friendly.

They had tea and muffins out of a silver dish round the sitting-room fire, the children, tired now, sitting crosslegged on the carpet before the fire. It was all very domestic and cosy. It was Anna who said: 'I wish we could do this every day, Daddy—we've never done it at home, have we?'

'No, darling, and I can't think why not. We must make a habit of it.'

They went back to Highgate then, driving against a stream of homegoing cars up the M4 and weaving a slow way through crowded streets.

As soon as they were indoors Mr Trentham, who had hardly spoken on their way back, went to his study and shut the door, and Sadie took the two children upstairs, tidied them for their supper and went along to the playroom, where they had a fast and furious game of Old Maid before they went down to the dining room.

There was no sign of Mr Trentham, but he appeared briefly as they sat at table, kissed his little daughters goodnight and then kissed Sadie too, in an absent minded manner, which made her distraite for the rest of the evening.

He wasn't at breakfast the next morning, Woodley mentioned discreetly that he had gone up to the BBC headquarters to discuss a script. 'Quite a business it is too, miss,' he confided, 'all these people sitting round a table, all having their say—something in the Middle East, I fancy, though Mr Trentham did tell me that he rather fancied doing one of these fashionable spy stories.'

'He must be very clever and know lots of people.'

'Indeed he does. I understand he's to give a party shortly, miss—you'll be able to meet some of them, I daresay. Actors and actresses and suchlike.' Woodley sniffed in a genteel fashion. 'Not really the master's type, if I may say so, Miss Sadie.'

'I expect they're very clever and amusing, Woodley. We're going to take Gladstone for a walk—can we do any shopping for Mrs Woodley?'

'I'll ask her. Anna and Julie like the shops—they were never allowed to do the shopping when Miss Murch was here. Such happy little things they are now, begging your pardon, miss.'

Sadie thought that was a compliment and beamed at him. 'I'm glad you think so, Woodley.'

It must have been almost eleven o'clock that evening before she saw Mr Trentham. She would have been in her room long since, but there had been a film on the TV she had wanted to see and she had stayed up. She was coming out of the sitting room when he came into the house.

'Still up, Sadie?' he wanted to know. 'Checking up on me?'

'Certainly not, Mr Trentham, I've been watching a film.' She crossed the hall to the stairs. 'I think Woodley has gone to bed,' she observed. 'Can I get you anything?'

'No, thanks, I'm surfeited with nut cutlets and bean shoots. Don't ever fall in love with a vegetarian, Sadie. Is there a fire in the sitting room still? Good, I shall sit by it and drink myself insensible.'

'Why?' asked Sadie.

'That's about the only way in which to expurge the last few hours.'

'You're upset. Wasn't she pretty enough?'

'Are you being pert?' he asked her, and then laughed. Sadie left the stairs and went towards him. She had guessed right, he had already had enough to drink; she had read somewhere that one could mop up too much alcohol by eating something. 'I shall make you a sandwich,' she told him, 'and bring you a cup of coffee.'

There was cold beef in the fridge, she made an outsize sandwich, heated the coffee and carried them back to the sitting room. Mr Trentham was lying on the sofa with his eyes closed. He opened them as she reached the sofa. 'Even if I hadn't been caught, hook, line and sinker long ago, I am now,' he told her. 'You are above rubies, Sadie.'

Sadie didn't answer. She put down the tray on a small table by the sofa, removed the whisky decanter to a distance and poked up the fire. Then she wished him goodnight and went upstairs to bed.

He was at breakfast when they got down the next morning, wished them a perfectly normal good morning, submitted to his daughters' hugs and once they had started on their porridge, suggested that they might all go to the Tower. 'Always provided that you eat all your breakfast and that Sadie will come with us.'

Breakfast had never been eaten so quickly, and since Sadie, in answer to his questioning look, had said that of course she'd love to go too, there was nothing to stop them leaving directly after breakfast. In the car Mr Trentham said: 'By the way, everyone's coming to the party. You'd better go and buy that dress tomorrow or my dear sister will take me to task. Do you know which shop it is?'

'Yes, I think so, your sister gave me the name.'

And after that he had no more to say until he had parked the car and they had been admitted. 'Let's get a Yeoman Warder to ourselves,' he suggested, and took Sadie's arm. 'And mind and listen to all that he has to say so that you can answer the children's questions later on.'

It was difficult to give her full attention with her arm tucked so comfortably in his. The Tower had been finished in the eleventh century, built by William the First and his son, used as a fortress and then encircled by two walls. They were led from one grim apartment to another, and the grimmer they were the more the children enjoyed it, asking bloodthirsty questions about the unfortunate people who had been imprisoned in them, looking at the names carved into the stone walls. Sadie found it all very sad, and was glad when they went to see the Crown Jewels. They were so magnificent that they didn't look real, but she gazed with the same rapt attention as the children. Mr Trentham, who had let go her arm, stood a little apart, watching her and smiling a little.

It was time for lunch by the time they were out in the modern world again. Mr Trentham took them back to the car and drove them to Mark Lane to the Viceroy Restaurant, where they ate a delicious meal, handsomely served, and discussed at great length all they had seen that morning. And Sadie found herself joining in with as much enthusiasm as the children, quite forgetting to be suspicious of Mr Trentham's smile—indeed, she smiled back at him so warmly that his bland good humour almost slipped; only his eyes gleamed each time he looked at her.

They got back home during the afternoon and since the children were still excited, Sadie suggested tea in the playroom, a short walk with Gladstone and to bed a little earlier than usual after their supper. Of Mr Trentham there was no sign. He had disappeared as he so often did, leaving no trace. Once the children were tucked up and asleep she went down for her own meal and then went to bed. It had been a lovely day as far as it went. She sighed and slept.

The next day, leaving the children with Teresa, she went to the boutique. She had money enough, for she had little enough to buy for herself. Now, with every penny she had in her purse, she walked into the shop, encouraged by the quite reasonable prices on the price tags in the window.

Lady Crawley had said green taffeta, and she went slowly along the rails firmly rejecting the sensible browns and greys hanging there. 'It has got to be green,' she told the pleasant woman in the shop, 'and taffeta…'

The woman looked doubtful. 'I might have something in the stockroom—our sale isn't till next week, but I could let you have it at sale price. You're a size ten, aren't you?'

She bustled away and came back with a dress over her arm. It wasn't taffeta, but it was a glowing green organza over a silk slip with a wide V neck and short tight sleeves. Sadie tried it on, staring at the image in the mirror; she looked quite different and she wasn't very happy about the neckline; it seemed a bit low, although the woman assured her that it was modest enough. But the rest was quite perfect. Sadie bought it, and since the woman had taken several pounds off its price, there was enough money to buy slippers.

She was lucky again, for the sales were still on. She browsed from one shoe shop to the next, making up her mind, and finally settled for bronze sandals because they would go very nicely with the amber crêpe too.

Back at the house, she had a dress rehearsal with the two little girls, Teresa and Mrs Woodley an admiring audience. They pronounced her purchases quite perfect and were sworn to secrecy not to say a word to anyone, something they found very difficult when they went downstairs to have tea with their father. They were almost bursting with their secrets, and only Sadie's warning glances stopped them from giving him hints.

'I'm to be surprised, I suppose. May I not have the smallest hint, Sadie?'

'Well, it's not a sack,' said Sadie, and went pink under his amused eyes.

He took himself out of the house the next day; the drawing room was being got ready for the dancing and Mrs Woodley was busy in the kitchen making canapés for the party, although she had told Sadie that there would be a van coming from Fortnum and Mason with party food. 'And Mr Trentham likes my sausage rolls,' she confided. 'I always make a good batch of those, he hasn't much patience with those fiddly bits and pieces.'

Sadie, anxious to help, had volunteered to do the flowers, and she and the children spent a happy morning arranging daffodils and hyacinths and narcissi and pots of cyclamen and even lilac. The florist's bill would be astronomical, and from what she had seen carried into the kitchen, so would the food bill. She didn't know much about drinks; probably that bill would be as much as the other two together.

They'd had a picnic lunch in order to leave Mrs Woodley free to make her canapés. They had tea round the fire in the sitting room and then, because the children were restless, she put on Gladstone's lead and took all three of them for a brisk walk round the square. By the time they got back it was to supper, baths and bed. She tucked them up, kissed them both, left Gladstone in charge and went along to get ready for the evening. There was still no sign of Mr Trentham and it was getting on for half past seven.

She had promised to do a last-minute round to make sure that everything was as it should be; she bathed and changed into the new dress, did her face, put her hair up in a neat chignon, and went downstairs.

They were fated to meet in the hall. Mr Trentham let himself in as she was halfway to the drawing room, and Sadie didn't stop. She said:

'Good evening, Mr Trentham, you'll have to hurry.'

He stood looking at her. 'This is hardly a hurrying moment,' he said softly.

'Stand still, Sadie. I want to look at you.'

CHAPTER NINE

SADIE FOUND HERSELF quite breathless. 'Your sister said green,' she said, 'and I said I'd just take a quick look round.'

He ignored this. 'I want to talk to you, Sadie.'

'Mr Trentham, you can't, you really must go and change.'

He tossed his coat on to a chair. 'I've waited so long, I can wait a little longer,' he observed, and then as he reached the stairs and prepared to go up them, 'You look beautiful, Sadie, I want you to remember that during the evening.' Half way up he turned. 'Are the children in bed?'

'Yes, but not asleep.'

'I'll go and see them before I change.'

There was no time to think about what he'd said. Sadie flew round the house, checking this and that, going to the kitchen to make sure that Mrs Woodley had everything ready and if there was anything she could do.

'Bless your heart, miss, no, everything is just fine. You look a treat for sore eyes, that you do— such a pretty dress too. You run along and enjoy yourself; they'll be arriving any minute now.'

Sadie retreated to the small sitting room. She might be in a pretty dress and a guest of Mr Trentham, but she was also his housekeeper. She would wait until almost everyone had arrived and then she would go into the drawing room.

She stayed there for almost half an hour, and not until the house was humming with voices did she cross the hall and slip into the drawing room, to be immediately pounced upon by Mr Trentham. 'Where on earth have you been? Come and meet a few people...'

She was passed from group to group, carefully noting names and faces, noting too the beautiful clothes and the jewels the women wore, and after a time she wished that Mr Trentham would let her slip away to a quiet corner instead of keeping her by his side; the men were kind enough, but the women looked at her with unfriendly eyes and called her darling when they didn't mean it.

But presently Mr Trentham was called away and she slipped away too. With any luck, she would be able to escape; but not just yet, it seemed. Someone had put the record player on and people were already dancing; a young man with a rather stupid face put out a hand and stopped her.

'Let's dance,' he said, and whisked her off to the centre of the room. Sadie had never had much chance to dance, but she was light on her feet and quick to learn. Mr Trentham, coming back into the room, saw her apparently enjoying herself and turned away with a small frown. A minute later he was dancing with Mrs Langley.

Judging from the noise, the party was a great success. By suppertime everyone was talking at the top of his or her voice; the record player was blaring and Woodley and Teresa were having their trays of drinks emptied as fast as they could fill them. Sadie, dancing with a short stout man who talked about nothing else but the films he produced, was beginning to get a headache. The man droned on and on and she sought feverishly for a good reason for leaving him. The children... She broke in on his account of a recent film he had made and told him very politely, in a voice full of regret, that she must really go and see if the children were all right.

'Take your duties seriously, don't you?' he asked slyly.

She missed the slyness. 'That's what I'm paid for,' she told him, and slipped away.

She shut the drawing-room door after her and sighed with relief. The sigh turned to a gasp as it was opened at once behind her and Mr Trentham joined her. 'And where are you off to?' he wanted to know.

'Just off to make sure the children are asleep.'

'You're not enjoying yourself, are you?'

She tempered her honesty with a white lie. 'Well, I'm not used to this—this kind of evening.'

'Not even in the line of duty?'

She said anxiously: 'I'm letting you down? I'm sorry, but you must know by now that I'm not witty or clever.' She added with a hint of bitterness: 'I'm not even a pretty lady.'

He took her hands. 'That isn't what I meant. You'll find it hard to believe, but I don't like this kind of an evening either. But it's part of my work; knowing everyone—that's what I meant—in the line of duty.'

Sadie stared up at him, puzzled. 'You mean because I work for you?'

He shook his head. 'I'd quite forgotten that. No, I hoped...' The door opened behind them and the short stout man came out.

'Children by any other name,' he said to Sadie, and dug her in the ribs, winking at her. 'You're a sly puss, aren't you, girlie?'

Mr Trentham's hand tightened on her arm. 'You're barking up the wrong tree, Sam. I'm sure you didn't mean a word of that.' His voice sent shivers down her spine and, from the look of him, down Sam's as well.

'No offence, just my fun—splendid young lady—my apologies.' He looked at Mr Trentham.

'Wanted to see you, old fellow, about that contract—it'll only take a couple of minutes of your
time.'

'Very well—Sadie, come down again when
you've seen to the children.'

She nodded and went upstairs. When she was out
of sight, Mr Trentham turned his attention to his
companion. 'My future plans are a bit uncertain,'
he observed coolly. 'What have you in mind?'

The children weren't asleep. Indeed, they had
never been more wide awake. They sat up in bed
and demanded to know what dresses the ladies were
wearing, what Sadie had eaten, had she danced, was
Daddy enjoying himself?

She answered their questions patiently and finally, because they wouldn't settle, let them put on
their dressing gowns and slippers and creep along
to the gallery with her and peep down through its
wrought iron railings.

There were several people in the hall now, going
to or coming from the dining room and the smaller
sitting room where the food was laid out.

'There's Miss Thornton in that pink dress,' whispered Anna, nipping Sadie's arm. 'She looks horrid—I do hope Daddy doesn't want to marry her.'

Sadie agreed with silent fervour.

'And there's Mrs Langley and Mrs Trevor talking to that fat man. There's no sign of Daddy—where is he?'

'With his guests,' whispered Sadie, and hoped with all her heart that he was. She had given the matter some careful thought and had come to the conclusion that although he made light of his lovely lady friends, he really was thinking of getting married to one of them; little things he had let fall…it didn't bear thinking about.

'Bed, darlings,' she whispered, and they all crept back and she tucked them up once more, giggling, but sleepy now. She sat down in a chair, glad of a few minutes' quiet, not wanting to go back downstairs but knowing that she would because Oliver had asked her to. And she mustn't think of him as Oliver; he must be Mr Trentham, now and always. Always? She went and peered at her face in the dressing table mirror. There was, she had to admit, absolutely nothing to attract a man in it.

Sadie made sure that the children were really asleep and went to the half open door, then paused. Two women were standing with their backs to her, gossiping, not attempting to lower their voices. It took her a couple of seconds to realise that they were discussing her and Mr Trentham.

'One wonders what he sees in her.' It was the younger of the two women who spoke, and Sadie dimly remembered meeting her earlier in the evening.

'But you know what a clever devil he is—she was only the housekeeper to start with, now she's tied up with the kids. He's charmed her into it, and that couldn't have been difficult; she's no beauty. I suppose she makes a change.'

They laughed together and the other, older woman said: 'Plain bread and butter between the cake, dear!'

'Plain's the word, darling. And I bet you that dress she's wearing is one he bought for her.' She laughed again, a spiteful sound. 'I wonder he shows her off in the way he does.'

'He's no fool; I heard that they're after him to write that documentary about the Middle East—you know the one I mean—very convenient for him, he's got her so enslaved with those kids of his that she'll stay to look after them until he feels like coming home again, then probably he'll hint at wedding bells just around the corner.'

'Not for her, though—Reggie told me in the strictest confidence that Oliver's planning to get married. This stupid creature from God knows where looks just the kind to love him for ever and give in to his every whim while he nips off with his bride.'

'Wonder who she is?'

'I've no idea—none of us have—haven't we all been trying to marry him for the last few years, and as far as I know, we've none of us succeeded in getting behind that suave charm.'

They began to stroll towards the stairs. 'All the same, I'd be willing to give it a whirl—marrying him. I often think we don't know him at all.'

The older woman's answer was lost as they went downstairs, leaving Sadie, very quiet, very white, standing by the door. She felt sick and near to tears, remembering every word of their conversation. Was that what Mr Trentham's friends thought of her? That she was a silly country girl, dazzled by his face and wealth, allowing him to pull the wool over her eyes until he found it convenient to sack her? And did he think of her in the same way? Did he laugh at her secretly? She couldn't believe that. She put her small determined chin up and went downstairs, and her heart lifted when he came across the room to meet her.

'Children all right?' he wanted to know. 'Sadie, I'm thinking of signing a contract for a script about the Middle East. This isn't the time or the place to discuss it, but they want some sort of an answer by the morning.'

So it was true; he was making use of her, because she knew now that he must have some idea of her feelings and was turning them to his own advan-

tage. She didn't want to believe it of him, but there
didn't seem any other answer, and here in the din
and bustle of the party, she couldn't think straight.
She didn't quite meet his eyes. 'What about the
children?'

'They're going to Cecilia for a day or two, they
can stay longer—you could go with them, it will
give you a break. We'll have to get them down to
the cottage in time for school, of course.' He smiled
at her and her heart rocked against her ribs. 'There's
a great deal of planning to do—that will have to
come presently.'

There was no need for her reply as they were
joined by the short fat man. He tapped Sadie on the
shoulder. 'Well, girlie, it all depends on you, you
know. What's it to be, yes or no?'

Mr Trentham interposed coldly: 'She's hardly
had time to make up her mind. I suggest we leave
it until the morning.' He looked at Sadie's sober
white face and gave a puzzled frown. 'We'll talk
about this later.' And when the man had gone away:
'What's happened, Sadie? Has someone said something to upset you?'

She choked on a lie, and shook her head instead.
Just in that last minute or two she had discovered
that she couldn't go on. She loved him and she had
grown fond of the children, but there was no happiness for her in a future where he was married to

someone else and she was the housekeeper, nanny, dwindling into her thirties, her forties. She would have to cut loose quickly, go right away. He could find another governess as well as someone to run the cottage, go to his Middle East job and marry this girl; for there was a girl, of that she was sure.

She was hardly aware of the rest of the evening. Presently people began to leave until the very last had gone through the doors and Woodley was locking up. It was late, but while her courage was high, she must settle the matter. And Mr Trentham made it easy for her, strolling out of the drawing room, his hands in his pockets, smiling.

'Thank God that's over! Shall we have a drink before we go to bed? And talk...'

'Nothing to drink, thank you, but I should like to talk.'

He came to a halt, the puzzled frown back again. 'Yes?'

'I should like to leave, Mr Trentham. I should like to go back to the cottage...'

He interrupted her. 'Homesick? Well, I'm afraid I'm tied up for a couple of days, but I'll drive you down as soon after that as possible.'

'You don't understand. I mean I want to leave— you and the children...'

His eyes narrowed. 'My dear girl, have you lost your wits or had too much sherry?'

Sadie shook her head. 'No. I'll go by train to-morrow, please. I'll pack my things there and go...'

'Where to?'

She looked away. 'I'll think of something.'

'And what about Tom?'

'I wondered if you would mind very much if he stayed at the cottage? The children love him and it's his home.'

'Yours too, Sadie.' His voice was very gentle.

She heaved a deep sigh. 'I've quite made up my mind—if you don't object, Mr Trentham.'

'Of course I object, and I want to know your reasons.'

'I'd rather not explain.'

'Then don't. I've no wish to force your confidence.' His voice was harsh. 'Presumably you have your excuses ready for the children—I thought you were fond of them, but I've been mistaken, as indeed I've been mistaken about other things. Make whatever arrangements you think fit—you may as well go tomorrow, I'll take the children to my sister's.'

He opened his study door and went inside without another word.

Sadie stood looking at the closed door. She only needed to take a few steps and open it and tell him about the gossiping women and ask him... What? If he loved her? That would be ridiculous. Whom he intended to marry? What was to become of her? Had he been jollying her along all these weeks for his own ends? She found that she couldn't do it. Presently she went upstairs and undressed, got her case from the closet and packed her things. The sooner she went now the better. There were the children to tell, of course, and that would be ghastly. She lay in bed rehearsing what she was going to say, and what she would say to Oliver, too. Presently, from sheer misery, she slept.

The little girls were blissfully unobservant of her white face and pink-tipped nose in the morning. They received her news with noisy regret, but since they believed she was only going for a few days while they visited their aunt, they cheered up quickly enough. Over the breakfast table Anna wanted to know if she couldn't go with them for a few days and then go to the cottage. 'You could, you know, Sadie,' she begged.

'Well, love, I thought it would be a good idea if I just popped down to the cottage and made sure that Tom was all right and get it a bit ready for your return, and there's a basket to get for Gladstone and some things to buy…'

It was a successful red herring, and presently they all went upstairs to pack the children's clothes, and Sadie, more than thankful that Mr Trentham hadn't been at breakfast, arranged their things.

But he was there in the hall when Teresa came to say that the children were to go down to their father, and since it would have invited questions from the children if she hadn't gone too, Sadie went with them. They shed a few tears as she kissed them goodbye, but cheered up quickly enough when she pointed out the grand time they were going to have at their Aunt's. And as for Mr Trentham, he preserved a bland countenance which betrayed none of his feelings, bidding her a polite goodbye as they left. She went back to her room and had a good cry, then washed her face, finished her packing and went to say goodbye to the Woodleys and Teresa. Mr Trentham had said that he wouldn't be back for lunch, but she dared not take the risk of seeing him again, so she got Woodley to get her a taxi and went to get her outdoor things.

It was then that she saw the envelope on her dressing room table, and she tore it open, hoping wildly that he had written to her. There was a month's salary inside, nothing more. It was a good thing that she hadn't the time to have another good cry—as it was, she was hard put to it not to do so as she left, for the Woodleys and Teresa seemed sad to see her go.

It was a long tiring journey, but she was lucky enough to catch the last afternoon bus to Chelcombe. It was dark as she began the walk up the lane to the cottage, and in the cold and the gloom as she went up the path, it looked far from welcoming. Moreover, she had forgotten all about food, and now, after nothing to eat all day, she was hungry.

She unlocked the door and went inside, switching on all the lights as she went through the house. There was tea, of course, and sugar and some tinned milk and some tins of soup. She made a meal of sorts, dragged her case upstairs, undressed, and armed with several hot water bottles, went to bed. She would have all the next day to sort things out, air the cottage and lay the fires ready for the children's return.

She hadn't expected to go to sleep, but she was so tired and unhappy that she could no longer think straight. Sleep overcame her before she had put two coherent thoughts together.

It was pitch dark and very cold when she woke up and she knew at once that something had woken her. She sat up in bed, the bedclothes up to her chin, and listened. The noise came again, very faint, a gentle scraping. Someone trying to open a window? She got out of bed, bundled on her dressing gown and slippers and opened her door. The noise had stopped; she crept down the landing to the head of the stairs and started cautiously down them. She was almost at the bottom when the light was put on, freezing her with fear so that her shriek was whispered.

Mr Trentham stood just inside the door, his sheepskin coat open over his dinner jacket. He looked tired, very tired, cross and at the same time satisfied about something.

'Aren't you going to ask me where I've been? You accused me once of never being home when I was wanted, but somehow I think I was right in thinking that I am wanted, Sadie. It is, of course, quite ridiculous that I should be forced to get up from a friend's dinner table, get into the car and come racing down here just to prove my point.'

Sadie came slowly down the rest of the stairs and stood in front of him.

'I don't understand—they said...'

'Ah, they—at the party, no doubt, dropping poisonous gossip into each other's ears for the lack of anything better to do. And you believed them? I'm surprised at you, Sadie—darling Sadie.'

She was so anxious to explain that the words came tumbling out without much sense. 'Well, you see, I wouldn't have, only when you said you'd been offered this job in the Middle East, and they said...'

He tossed his jacket into a corner and pulled her close. 'My darling girl, I don't want to hear what they said. They don't exist in our world; you should never believe all you hear.'

'I tried not to, but they said you were going to get married, and—oh, Oliver, I couldn't bear that…'

'Well, you'll have to learn to, sweetheart, because you're the girl I'm marrying and if you hadn't been so busy being a housekeeper and mothering the children, you'd have seen that for yourself.'

'Oh, Oliver!'

He kissed her then, long and soundly, but presently she lifted her head.

'The children, and Gladstone and Tom…'

'The children and Gladstone will stay at Cecilia's until we're married. Tom will come here, of course, just as soon as we return here.'

'But the job in the Middle East?'

'I've said I can't do it for six months at least—family commitments.'

'Oh, but that little fat man…'

'Quiet,' said Oliver, and fell to kissing her again.

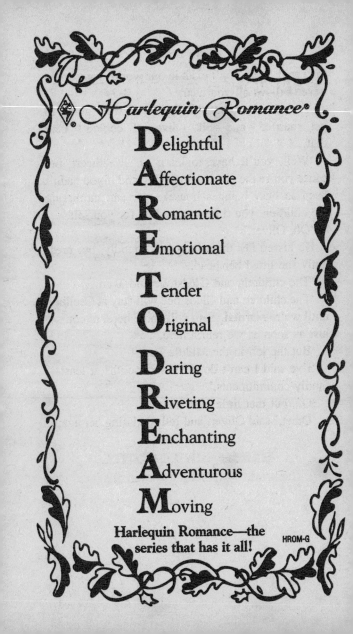

Harlequin Romance®

Delightful

Affectionate

Romantic

Emotional

Tender

Original

Daring

Riveting

Enchanting

Adventurous

Moving

Harlequin Romance—the
series that has it all!

HROM-G

HARLEQUIN ✦ PRESENTS®

HARLEQUIN PRESENTS
men you won't be able to resist
falling in love with...

HARLEQUIN PRESENTS
women who have feelings
just like your own...

HARLEQUIN PRESENTS
powerful passion in
exotic international settings...

HARLEQUIN PRESENTS
intense, dramatic stories that will keep you
turning to the very last page...

HARLEQUIN PRESENTS
The world's bestselling romance series!

Harlequin® Historical

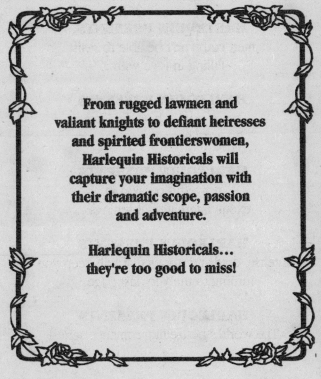

From rugged lawmen and
valiant knights to defiant heiresses
and spirited frontierswomen,
Harlequin Historicals will
capture your imagination with
their dramatic scope, passion
and adventure.

Harlequin Historicals...
they're too good to miss!

HHGENR